P9-BZI-260

# HER HEART
# FOR THE ASKING

# HER HEART FOR THE ASKING

•

## Lisa Mondello

*AVALON BOOKS*
NEW YORK

**3 3113 02061 9690**

PRINTED IN THE UNITED STATES OF AMERICA
ON ACID-FREE PAPER
BY HADDON CRAFTSMEN, BLOOMSBURG, PENNSYLVANIA

Thanks and big hugs to my family for their constant love and support, and to Natalie, Cathy, Karen and Carolyn for always being there.

This book is dedicated to my dear friend Natalie Damschroder. I never could have done this one without you if you hadn't been there for all the others.

## Chapter One

"What are you doing here?" Mandy Morgan asked, dropping her too-heavy overnight case on the sun-roasted tarmac. After a grueling forty-eight-hour work stint and a five-hour flight from Philadelphia, she stood wilting under the brutal Texas sun, facing her biggest nightmare.

*Beau Gentry.*

She groaned inwardly, drinking Beau in with her eyes like she hadn't had a drop of water in months. *Eight years was more like it.* If she were eight years smarter she would be moving her aching feet as fast as she could in the opposite direction. But all she could do was stare at eyes so bright they rivaled the blazing sun. At lips so kissable she'd spent the better part of her adult life trying to wipe the memory clean from her mind.

She had expected Beau would have aged some. When she allowed herself to think about him at all, she reminded herself. The faint lines etched in the corners of his sleepy gray-blue eyes gave a hint of maturity, but most probably were caused by long days in the cruel sun.

She fought the urge to take a closer look at his ruggedly handsome features, but failed. How could he have gotten better looking after being abused by every bronc-busting horse on the rodeo circuit? His angular jaw, strong and determined, was shaded with beard growth that was probably a day old, maybe more. Mandy suspected that if Beau grew a full beard, it would grow in thick and be the smooth texture of his almost black head of hair. She forced aside the past memories that gave her such knowledge with renewed irritation.

*The man didn't even have the decency to have a crooked nose.* What should have been bent and awkward from being broken a few too many times was instead long and straight, shaped perfectly between high cheekbones most women would swoon over, or kill to have themselves. But on Beau Gentry, it was just one thousand percent robust cowboy.

*Darn him.*

"I'm your ride out to the Double T," Beau said, gripping the edge of his white straw cowboy hat and tipping it in a cordial gesture.

She ground the heels of her low pumps into the soft tar to contain her growing irritation. *Did he think she was an idiot?* "No way."

" 'Fraid so," he said, his expression slightly askew.

"Hank didn't mention anything about you coming to get me when I spoke to him on the phone."

"I suspect he thought you would have found some excuse not to come if you knew I was picking you up."

"He would have been right. Why didn't one of the hands come get me?"

Settling his hand at the base of his neck, Beau replied, "You're looking at him. As of three weeks ago I am one of the ranch hands at the Double T."

*What?!* Mandy fought the urge to keep her surprise from showing, but immediately failed. Beau Gentry was the son of her uncle's biggest rival. It hadn't stopped her from falling head over heels for the man on those long, lazy summers she had come down to the ranch to visit her aunt and uncle. Of course, back then rodeo was all Beau cared about, not his father's spread. Not her, she remembered painfully.

He was going to go PRCA and be a world champion. It was his dream and all he ever talked about. He was good enough to do it, too, Mandy thought wryly. So good, he hadn't given her a second glance when he rode out of Texas without her eight years ago on the heels of a golden sunset.

Her chuckle was almost hysterical. "You really expect me to leave this airport with you?"

"That was the plan," he said, smiling, his gray eyes seeing more of her than she wanted him to see. He held his ground. He had to know how difficult it was for her to see him after all this time. It didn't matter that he didn't share her unrest. He could have at least had the decency to think about her feelings. But then he hadn't thought about her feelings eight years ago when he broke her heart, so it didn't seem he was any more inclined to do so now.

Beau Gentry might be clueless, but there was no way Mandy was going anywhere with him. No way she'd spend the next two hours bouncing up and down in a hot pickup truck, breathing in his scent and wrestling with memories. . . .

Mandy twisted on her heels and surged in the opposite direction. "Forget it," she called over her shoulder.

There had to be a cab going somewhere.

Anywhere. A hot, sticky bus would be a lot more inviting than spending the next few hours in inescapable close quarters with Beau.

"Mandy, what are you going to do, walk all the way to the Double T?"

"I'm sorry you were dragged out here like this, Beau. But I'm afraid it was a waste of your time. I . . . can rent a car."

Behind her, Mandy heard his heavy sigh and the sound of his boots stopping short on the tarmac. *Defeat? Regret?* She wasn't sure, but she was very sure she shouldn't care.

Since Mandy had just come off a forty-eight-hour work marathon and had let her cell phone battery run down, she concentrated on finding a pay phone.

"It's been a while since you've been around. The car rental service went belly up here two years ago. About the closest thing you could do to get away from me right now is to take a cab to the bus depot. And I'll just have to pick you up when you get to Steerage Rock anyway."

She stopped walking when she reached the pay phone just outside the small terminal, angling back to see where Beau was standing. The airport was small enough not to have gates. Everyone got dropped off on the tarmac. She glanced past the booth to the boarded-up window near the entrance to the small building that housed both the air tower, the terminal, and a small restaurant—a fast-food diner of sorts. The peeled paint of the weather-beaten banner didn't hide the letters of a rental car company that indeed had gone out of business.

She blew out an exasperated breath of frustration in the already hot Texas heat. She wasn't ready to give up. Right now a bus looked as if it might be a possibility, since the last orange taxi had just pulled out of the parking lot with one of the passengers who'd been on the same flight she'd taken. She remembered seeing a bus depot not far from here when Uncle Hank used to pick her up. It wouldn't take her all the way to the Double T, but close enough not to put Uncle Hank or Aunt Corrine out when she called and asked for a ride.

She was being ridiculous. Part of her knew that, accepted her behavior as being childish. But part of her rationalized it as necessary. She knew all too well the dangers of being with Beau Gentry. It had taken Mandy too long to get over him, and she wasn't about to allow the man and his charms to seep into her heart again.

"I can manage," she said resolutely.

"I suspect you could. You seem to have done fine for yourself, judging by the fancy clothes you're wearing and that designer luggage."

With a fistful of quarters in her palm, she

swung around, cradling the phone in her other hand. Leveling him with a warning stare, she said tightly, "I don't think you're in a position to judge me after what you did."

His face showed a momentary flash of regret. "That was a long time ago, Mandy."

She gripped the quarters in her hand, feeling her pulse hammer in her wrist. "I have a long memory."

Turning her attention back to the task at hand, Mandy decided the phone book was useless. What was the company name on the side of that yellow cab? It had been eight years since she'd been in Texas. Eight years was a long time for a county to change. Who could she possibly call if her one-and-only ally in Texas sent the one man she swore she'd never lay eyes on again?

Defeated, she dropped the out-of-date phone book, and chided herself for not charging her cell phone before she left for the airport. She had most of her numbers on speed dial and couldn't even recall the number for the Double T. That would teach her never to let her cell phone battery run down again, leaving her unprepared.

"Tell me, Beau. Why did you come here? Someone else could have easily come for me. Why did it have to be you?"

His gray-blue eyes lost some of their luster and grew solemn. There was a time long ago when she thought she could stare at those eyes and be lost in them for hours. *I still could,* she realized with sudden regret.

Not a good sign.

He adjusted his hat in that lazy way he always did. "Because Hank asked me to. That's why."

There was her life in a nutshell. Beau was asked. And Mandy wasn't. Mandy was never asked, she was told. And like the good girl she was raised to be, Mandy always complied.

She thought back to the conversation she'd had with her mother just three days ago with renewed irritation.

"I'm not asking, Mandy," Leandra Morgan had said over the phone.

*I'm telling you.*

Her mother didn't actually have to say the last part for Mandy to know what she was thinking. It was a given. It followed every request the woman ever made. *I'm not asking you to keep your tongue. I'm not asking you to come to your cousin's party. I'm not asking you to apologize to your father. I'm not asking you to work for the family business . . . or date the son of your father's biggest client. I'm telling you.*

Three days ago Mandy had sat in her downtown Philadelphia office on the phone with her mother, impatiently drumming her foot on the lift on her chair. "I am knee-deep in this project for Dad, Mom. There's just no way I'm going to be able to get away. I can't make both of you happy at the same time."

"You'll just have to find a way." Leandra's voice came like static over the phone. "Your uncle . . . isn't himself. It's been a long time since you've visited him in Texas. I think it would do him some good to see you again. I think it's time you go."

A tug of emotion had squeezed her chest. It had been years since she'd visited Uncle Hank and Aunt Corrine at the Double T. She'd never told her mother why she'd stopped her summer visits, and thankfully, her mother had never pushed for a reason. Mandy suspected her mother had just accepted her decision not to make her summer vacation as her daughter's way of asserting adolescent independence— wanting to remain in Philadelphia to enjoy some summer freedom with her friends. She'd never spoken about what happened that last summer. Never confided in anyone about her first love. And that was just fine with Mandy. She didn't need to be reminded.

"I'll call Uncle Hank and explain. I can't get away now. He'll understand," she'd said.

"You make it happen, young lady." *I'm not asking.*

A voice boomed over the outdoor loud-speaker, announcing the arrival of another flight. Mandy was immediately pulled back to the present, back to Texas and the hot tarmac she now stood on, heels sinking into the sun-softened tar.

"We've got a couple of hours ahead of us. I'm going to get something cold to drink for the ride," Beau said, ambling toward the building. Turning back, he asked, "You want something?"

*Yeah, I want you to go away. I want to forget the way you broke my heart all those years ago.* But she knew that was futile. She'd been a fool to think she'd gotten over him. If eight years and countless dates with very eligible men hadn't exorcised the memory of Beau Gentry from her heart and soul, nothing would.

Mandy glanced at him, defeat sitting just beneath the surface of her composure, and shook her head.

How could he act so normal? How could he be asking her something as simple as whether she wanted a soda, when the last time they'd seen each other had been such a sham?

*And how dare he be so handsome after a two-hour ride in a hot pickup truck?* His white T-shirt stretched taut across his muscled shoulders. She knew firsthand just how strong those arms were when they were wrapped around her in a warm embrace. After years of breaking every wild bronc on the circuit, they were sure to be even stronger.

There wasn't an ounce of body fat on the man. His jeans weren't a tight fit, even baggy in a few places. But on Beau, there was nothing sloppy about it. Just high-voltage sex appeal that had her pounding heart doing an acrobatic dance right there on the blazing tarmac.

*And he was nonchalantly asking if she wanted a soda.*

The door closed behind him as he stepped into the building, and Mandy watched through the tinted window while he wandered over to the soda machine in the corner and made his selection. He stood there, his weight shifted lazily to one hip in a devil-may-care way.

She tore her gaze away from her torturer. Beau Gentry might look like a dream come true from the cover of *Modern Cowboy,* but she was an utter disaster after her long flight.

Suddenly aware she was still wearing yesterday's silk suit, she ran her hands down her skirt in a futile attempt to smooth out the wrinkles. Giving up, she rummaged through her purse for a barrette and a comb. Anything to pull together hair that had become unruly from neglect, heat, and the wind. Settling on a hair band and her fingers as a comb, she wrestled her normally-wavy-gone-curly-in-the-heat dusty blond hair into a ponytail. She hated that it made her look sixteen again, but there wasn't much she could do until she could get back to the ranch and unpack her things.

As Mandy watched Beau walk out into the sunshine with two root beers and a bag of chips in his hand, she reasoned she wasn't as vulnerable as she had been so many years ago. Letting the likes of Beau Gentry stomp on her heart was something she wouldn't do ever again. She was a woman now. She could do this. She led corporate business meetings. She used her innovative ideas to dazzle prospective clients into spending millions of advertising dollars with her father's firm. She'd just purchased an elegant townhouse in one of the trendiest sections of Philadelphia. All she had to do was pull herself together and she could handle this situation like the professional she was.

"I'm not going," she said, cursing inwardly for sounding like a spoiled child. *So much for the corporate executive touch.*

Beau's lips curled into a slight grin. He wouldn't win any points if he ticked Mandy off by laughing at the way her chin tilted up in defiance. That hadn't changed much. Or the flash of fire in her deep brown eyes. They still looked as black, and contrasted wildly with the natural streaks of blond in her hair. He'd always found that appealing, and adorable as all get-out. Already his fingers itched to let the soft curls of her hair tumble in his hand.

But she had changed. Any fool could see that Mandy Morgan had blossomed into a five-star beauty while he'd been out roaming the country these last eight years.

She was still as slim as she had been at sixteen, but her figure had filled out in all the places that made a man take notice. The light tilt in her hips that had taunted him when she was sixteen had matured into a graceful sway he found hypnotizing. Although she'd chewed off most of her lipstick, he noticed she now wore a slight hint of makeup on her cheeks and eyes, giving her the more exotic look of a woman.

And she still had the power to make his head spin like a lasso chasing a calf. He longed to see her smile again, hear her laugh bubble up from her soul. But given the way things had ended between them, and the way she stood before him now with her arms knotted tightly in front of her chest, her jaw set, he knew she wouldn't crack a smile just to spite him.

*Lord only knew why Hank insisted he be the one to pick her up at the airport.*

"Did you hear me?" she finally said, when he didn't answer her.

"Yeah, I did."

Her dark eyes widened slightly. "Oh. Good."

Beau reached down and picked up her leather garment bag, watching as her bewildered eyes followed his movement.

"It doesn't change anything though. Hank asked me to pick you up at the airport and bring you home, and that's what I'm doing if I have to toss you over my shoulder and drop you in the pickup."

Mandy gasped. "You wouldn't dare!"

"Wanna try me?" He couldn't help but smile. She just looked too darlin' getting all hot and flustered. She had to know he wouldn't give up. Not just because she was virtually stuck, and knew it, but because she knew he would never refuse Hank's request.

She sighed and closed her eyes. "You touch me and I'll . . ."

"What?"

"I'll . . ."

"Afraid of what you'll do?" His smile widened just thinking. "Or are you afraid of how you'll feel in my arms again?"

A veil of pain hooded her delicate features.

She wasn't just defeated, he realized. She still hurt after all these years. Guilt stabbed at his gut just thinking of how she was going to feel when she finally reached the Double T and she learned the real reason she had been called back to Texas.

Somehow, on those long drives from rodeo to rodeo the past eight years, Beau had fantasized about Mandy forgiving him one day for what he'd done. Maybe even understanding why he'd had to do it. As the years went on, he figured she'd have forgotten all about what the two of them had shared that summer, and moved on with her life. He didn't want to think of her finding comfort with another man, forgetting the way she used to melt like butter in his arms, the way they breathlessly clung to each other to steal just one more kiss before turning in each night. But it would have been easier for her if she had.

Looking in her haunted eyes now, Beau realized that was truly a fantasy. Her pain was still as raw as the day he'd left her eight years ago.

He gripped the bag of chips he'd just bought from the vending machine so hard it popped.

"Look, we have a long ride ahead of us. If you want, you can blast the radio with any station you want and pretend someone else is driving."

"You'll just start whistling to remind me you're there," she said, staring at the ground.

She remembered. Every trip to the local rodeos he'd been pent-up with anticipation. She liked to listen to the radio in the truck, and when he was nervous, he'd whistle, and it annoyed the tar out of her. But she teased him anyway, telling him if he was going to whistle, he could at least do it in key.

Having her remember that one small detail gave him a slice of hope. No, they'd never be able to pick up where they'd left off eight years ago. That part of his life was dead and buried. But maybe he'd have a chance to repair the damage he'd done. Maybe they could be friends.

Mandy threw her purse over her shoulder and headed toward the parking lot, leaving him to deal with her luggage. His eyes were drawn again to the graceful sway of her slender hips and the memory of her silky soft lips against his.

Being friends with Mandy as a consolation prize to having her in his arms did nothing to dispel the loneliness he suddenly felt in seeing her again after all these years. But it would have to do.

## Chapter Two

$B$eau carefully settled Mandy's suitcase in the back of the pickup, mindful to cover it with a thick tarp to protect it from the hot sun. Mandy didn't wait for him to extend his Texas charm by opening the door for her. Instead, she climbed into the cab herself and practically slammed the door in his face.

He supposed he deserved that. She wasn't happy about being forced into this position any more than he was.

Hank had asked him to pick Mandy up at the airport that morning. The past three weeks Beau had been at the Double T, Hank had made no mention of Mandy at all except to say that she was doing well. And he had only offered that

17

little tidbit of information when Beau's curiosity had won out and he had finally asked Hank directly about her.

Hank had to have known Mandy was on his mind. It was no secret to anyone that he and Mandy had been an inseparable pair that summer they were together. But Hank had never uttered a word, even a month ago when he called Beau asking for help.

After all the things Hank Promise had done for Beau, Hank had only ever asked two favors of him. It wasn't the most opportune time for him to drop everything. Some of the best rodeos were lined up ahead of him. He'd been in top form all year, and he knew this year he had a shot at winning the World Championship. He'd won other championships before, competed against the world's best, but he had never managed to win the title for himself. This year was his year. He was sure of it.

But then Hank had tracked him down while he was on the road. His old friend would never had made such a request if it wasn't awfully important. Beau owed all he knew about rodeo to Hank Promise. In many ways, Hank had formed him into a man far more than his old man had, much to Beau's dismay. Maybe if Mike Gentry's vendetta against Hank buying the Double T hadn't been so strong, Beau wouldn't have been so drawn to it in the first place.

Regardless, here he was eight years after walking out of his father's home, after walking out of Mandy's life in search of world fame and fortune on the rodeo circuit. It had torn him apart to leave her behind, but in an ironic twist of fate he'd come full circle. He was back in Texas, back at the Double T, with Mandy Morgan by his side.

Only this time, instead of loving him with all her heart and soul, she despised him.

Jamming the key into the ignition, Beau gunned the engine. Mandy was sitting so far on the other end of the wide bench seat she was pressed against the door. He turned on the radio to hide his disappointed sigh as he pulled out of the airport parking lot.

Was this what it was going to be like? With him living in the bunkhouse, working at the Double T, and Mandy living in the house, they were bound to run into each other. And if Hank was serious about his plans, they'd be running into each other a great deal.

They'd only gone a few miles on the interstate when Mandy leaned forward and switched off the radio. Beau took his eyes off the road only long enough to glance at her and see that she was staring at him. Questions shadowed her deep brown eyes, making her appear almost lost.

"Why did you really come back, Beau?" she asked softly.

"I told you. Hank asked me to."

"That's it?"

He nodded, making sure his right hand was firmly on the steering wheel while he draped his left along the open window.

"And you just said yes? Just like that. You just dropped everything and decided to come running back to Steerage Rock after years of staying away?"

Beau heard the unspoken question, even if she didn't say it aloud. *Was the reason you hadn't come back in eight years to avoid seeing me?* That was a little harder to answer than the rest. He hadn't come back to Steerage Rock for a lot of reasons. Partly because he didn't want to keep hashing out why he wasn't settling down and working the Silverado Cattle Company with his father. Mike Gentry never understood anyone else's goals but his own. There wasn't a way in the world his old man would ever understand why he couldn't work alongside him at the ranch.

Beau had reconciled himself to that long ago. He'd tried to be what his father wanted. He'd learned all about ranching with the intent of one day taking over the family spread with his three brothers. But it had never been his dream.

Beau had had the fever for rodeo even before that first time he'd ridden over the pasture trying to steal a peek at the Double T when he was ten years old, just to see what his dad was fussing and fuming about. He'd never understood his father's vendetta against Hank Promise, but he understood the fever for riding a wild bronc. And with Hank's help, he'd become one of the best bronco bareback riders on the circuit.

"Yeah, Mandy, Hank said he needed me and I left everything behind. I owe him a lot."

Shaking her head, she stared out the window, averting her gaze. She had her elbow pressed against the door and her fist tucked under her chin. Every so often a gust of wind whipped wayward strands of hair that had fallen from her ponytail around her face, and she briskly pushed them away.

Silence dragged on for a few minutes, and Beau contemplated turning the radio on again to drown out his hammering heart and the vacant sound of tires eating up the miles of road ahead. Then Mandy spoke again.

"I can't imagine why my uncle would forgive you for what you did. I told him, you know. Right after you left. I told him the real reason you'd been hanging around the Double T. You must have done some smooth talking to get back into his good graces."

"Hank doesn't harbor any bad feelings for what's happened over the years."

She snapped her gaze back to him. "What makes you so sure?"

"Mandy, it was no secret my father lived and breathed to make Hank's life miserable. It wasn't going to work, of course, because Hank's not that kind of man. Dad had never gotten over the fact that Hank outbid him for the Double T all those years ago. He always wanted that spread as his own and Hank knew it."

"Uncle Hank bought the Double T fair and square."

"I know that and you know that. If my father wasn't so stubborn he'd probably see that, too. But after all these years, I doubt that will ever happen. It would have been a lot better if ol' man Barrows hadn't promised he'd sell the land to dad before he died. Once the family and lawyers got hold of the estate, none of that mattered."

"Then why did Hank ask you to come back when he knows . . ."

"Despite what you think, I'm not the enemy. If it's good enough for Hank, why can't it be good enough for you?"

A cold cloud swiftly covered her features. "You know it's different," she answered quietly.

He glanced back at the vacant roadway ahead. "Yeah, maybe you're right. Why didn't you ever come back?"

"How do you know I didn't?"

"I've been at the Double T for three weeks now. Cowboys may not say much, but when they do, they're direct. You remember Mitch? He started working as a hand the last summer you visited the ranch."

"Vaguely. Lanky kid with freckles?"

Beau couldn't help but laugh. "Well, I wouldn't exactly call him lanky, but he remembers you quite fondly and mentioned you hadn't been back. How come?"

"What do you want this time?" she asked, ignoring his question.

It was his turned to be confused. "What do you mean?"

"You must want something if you're giving up everything you love, everything you've worked so hard for just to come back to Steerage Rock to work as a cowpoke for my uncle. Come on now, Beau. You have a shot at World Champion this year. It had to be something big."

His lips curled into a slow grin, earning him

a bigger scowl from Mandy. "You keeping tabs on me?"

"Never mind. Forget I asked."

He should, Beau thought. It wasn't a good idea to be flattered she'd gone to lengths to find out how he'd been doing. And it wasn't his place to reveal to her the real reason he'd come home from the circuit. Even if it was only for a short time. But something deep inside told him he'd be repeating the mistakes of the past if he didn't at least warn her. He'd kept his mouth shut eight years ago because it had been the right thing to do. This was different. This time they were talking about Hank's life.

"What made you come back after all this time?" he asked, figuring if there was even the slightest chance she knew something, he could unload the rest. After all, she'd come running, too.

"Mom said Uncle Hank hasn't been himself. It's been a while since I've come out for a visit and she thought it would help lift his spirits a little. Although I can't imagine how."

"I think she's right."

Mandy stared at him for a long moment, much like she used to do years ago when she was deciding whether to tell him a secret or keep it to herself. Back then she'd always end up climbing right across the cab, turning his head and kissing him right while he was driving. He'd end up swerving across the road recklessly until his heart stopped pounding and she settled next to him in the middle of the seat.

His heart pumped furiously now just with the memory. Those were foolishly wild times for them, when all he cared about was having Mandy Morgan in his arms as he rode from one local rodeo to the next. *Recklessly passionate times they'd shared.*

But this time, she wasn't climbing across the seat to saddle up next to him. This time Mandy just stared, a wariness flooding her expression. Her voice was grave as she spoke. "What aren't you telling me, Beau Gentry?"

He hesitated. In a few hours she was going to hear the truth anyway. What did it matter if he was the one to tell her? The least he could do was warn her. Give her time to come to grips before she saw her uncle.

"It's Hank's heart," he said quickly.

Her small gasp had his chest constricting. He longed to reach across the seat and touch her. To give her an ounce of comfort for the fear she must be feeling. But he knew comfort from him was probably the last thing she'd accept.

"Hank's always been healthy as a horse."

"I know."

"H-how bad?"

He swallowed as he glanced at her. Her eyes had filled with moisture, but her tears remained unshed. "He needs surgery bad or he won't make it."

"Oh, God." She buried her face in her hands. "Why didn't anyone tell me? Why didn't Uncle Hank or Aunt Corrine . . . or my mother tell me?"

"Does it matter? You know now."

"When is he going in for surgery?"

"That's just it, he's not."

"What? You just said he needed surgery or he'll . . . die."

"I suspect that may be why your mother wanted you to come so badly, to talk some sense into him. He has this foolish idea that he'll go when the Good Lord says it's his time. He wants nothing to do with bypass."

"But that's ridiculous. People have bypass surgery all the time and live normal, healthy lives for years afterwards. Why would he risk his life like this?"

"I'm not sure, but no matter what anyone tries to tell him, he insists he's not going under the knife. Maybe he'll listen to you."

Determination flared up in her tear-filled eyes. "You'd better believe it. I can't believe he's being this foolish."

"I'll probably get my hide chewed out when

we get back to the Double T for me telling you like this, but at least it won't be a shock when you finally get there."

The sound of the truck's tires rolling down the highway filled the air between them. Mandy stared vacantly out the window as the breeze blew the tendrils of hair framing her face about in a wild fury.

"Have you tried talking to him?" she asked quietly, after a few moments had passed.

Beau nodded. "I tell you, he's not listening to anyone."

The rest of the ride was made in silence. They didn't talk, they didn't listen to the radio, and he didn't whistle. Oh, he was anxious all right. Just being with Mandy had him on edge, ready to jump out of his skin more than any wild bronc ever could.

But he knew Mandy needed to be alone with her thoughts. Needed time to come to grips with what she'd face before they made it back to the Double T. Coming home had a way of doing that to you. But then he realized, the Double T had never really been Mandy Morgan's true home.

Mandy gazed at the long stretch of road ahead, the rolling pastures of grazing cattle, and endless fields of corn on either side of the road.

Uncle Hank was sick. Good Lord, he had the biggest heart of any man she knew and now his heart was failing him.

She should have known that. Beau Gentry shouldn't have been the one to tell her something so important.

Guilt consumed her for not staying more in touch with him and Aunt Corrine. The last time she'd seen them was when she'd graduated from college. They'd come up to Boston to attend her graduation from Boston University, but had only stayed on a day more before returning to Texas. Mandy had been anxious to get on with the graduation celebration with her friends from school before she had to go back to Philadelphia and start her job at her father's advertising firm.

They'd spoken on the phone every few months since then. She loved Uncle Hank like family, even though she knew he and Aunt Corrine weren't actual blood relations, but rather close family friends.

The front gate of the Double T, named after a particularly favorite horse from the rodeo circuit called Double Trouble, came into view. Mandy recalled the first time she'd come to Texas when she was only nine years old. Her mother had accompanied her and stayed for a few days, although it was evident being on a cattle ranch was the last place her mother wanted to be. Before that, Uncle Hank and Aunt Corrine had always come to Philadelphia to visit.

Her parents had thought it was time to broaden Mandy's horizon, let her know a different kind of life than the one she'd led in Philadelphia. But she was just a kid, and what did she know about horizons or cattle ranches or cities other than being with people she loved and with whom she felt safe?

Her mother stayed a few days that first visit and then told her she'd be spending the summer with her Uncle Hank and Aunt Corrine all by herself. Mandy had wrapped her arms around her mother's neck, refusing to let her mother leave her behind in Texas. But her mother told her she had to stay. *I'm not asking.* Mandy had no choice.

She'd spent every summer after that until she was sixteen. *Until Beau broke her heart and destroyed what dreams she dared to dream.*

Mandy always knew when it was time for a visit to Texas. Her parents would fight endlessly for weeks on end. Dad would work all kinds of hours, snap at everyone for every little thing. Her parents lived in the same house, but not together in any way that mattered. But when she returned from those summer vacations in Texas, she saw the positive change in their marriage. They'd hold hands and sneak kisses in the kitchen when they thought she wasn't looking.

As she got older and began to understand the workings of a relationship between a man and a woman, Mandy began to view her summer trips to Texas as time for her parents to rebuild whatever was breaking down in their marriage. She stopped resenting them for sending her away and even began looking forward to her summers at the Double T.

Mandy closed her eyes and tried to squash the foreboding feeling building up inside her. She glanced at Beau, who had surprised her by giving her some space during the long ride to collect herself.

He'd surprised her by asking why she hadn't returned to Texas. He'd known and said as much at the airport. But she hadn't answered him. Why hadn't she? She could have told him that she was busy going to college, making a career for herself. It was true to a certain point. She didn't have to tell him that the real reason was that she feared running into him again. After all, his family did own the adjoining spread, and if she spent any time outside the Double T, there was a possibility she'd bump into him if he was home.

Or she could have simply said that she'd

moved on with her life just as easily as he had when he rode out of Texas without her. Looking at him now, feeling the dull ache in her heart build with each passing second, she knew that wasn't true. Beau would see right through any attempt to state otherwise.

The ranch hadn't changed much. The outbuildings that had once seemed so enormous to Mandy as a child looked smaller, fragile even, and in need of some repair. The two-story farmhouse had some peeling paint on the front porch soffits, but other than that looked as inviting as it always had with its brick walkway, and hanging flower baskets lining the wraparound porch. The wicker rocking chairs that had once filled the front porch were replaced by a wide porch swing and a wooden glider built for two.

Before the truck had even rolled to a stop in front of the main house, Uncle Hank had thrown open the screen door and planted himself on the top porch step, holding his arms wide open for her. His smile was so bright, it made her chest ache.

Mandy couldn't help herself. With the weight of tears burning her eyes, she bolted from the cab and launched herself up the porch steps into Hank's arms. Hank folded her into a tight embrace and kissed her forehead.

"Oh, pretty little lady, I've missed you," he said.

"I'm sorry I haven't been to visit for a while," she started to say, but he waved her off.

"We'll have none of that. I'm just tickled to see you now. Come on in. Corrine is in the studio, but she told me to get her the second you arrived."

Mandy started to turn back to the truck. "I need to get my bags."

"I'll bring them in," Beau called out. "Just go say your hellos."

Arm in arm they walked through the narrow hallway leading to a small addition built on the back of the farmhouse. Aunt Corrine was an artist. It didn't matter what kind you called her. She created art in all shapes, sizes and mediums depending on which way the muse struck her or what supplies were on sale at the craft store—take your pick. Uncle Hank liked to encourage her creativity, saying if digging her hands in clay or plaster was enough to keep a sophisticated woman like Corrine by his side on a small Texas ranch, it was okay by him.

"Is she still working on aluminum sculptures?" Mandy asked quietly before they reached the studio.

"Nope. She's painting now. Calls them oils and uses her hands instead of brushes. Says it gives her more control. But I tell you true, it all ends up looking like finger painting to me," he said, chuckling.

"Mandy?" Corrine called out from inside the studio. "Is that you already, doll?"

"It sure is," Hank said.

Aunt Corrine appeared in the doorway, wearing a paint splattered smock that looked as if it might have been originally orange beneath all the paint. Her hands were indeed covered with gobs of thick blue, green, yellow, and red oil paint swirled together to make streaks. When she met Mandy's gaze she smiled and furiously started wiping her hands on her already filthy smock.

"I wasn't talking about you, Hank, and you know it," Corrine said, yanking the smock off and hanging it on a hook with some others that were just as colorful. Now fairly devoid of paint splatterings, she opened her arms to give Mandy a hug. "Honey, I can't believe how much you've grown."

Mandy couldn't help but laugh. "That's only because every time you see me you expect me to still be nine. How are you, Aunt Corrine?"

"Missing you, that's how. Come, let me show you what I've been working on."

Over the years Aunt Corrine's hobby had turned into more of a profession of sorts for her.

She hadn't made a whole lot of money off the sale of her work, but she had had a showing in Dallas a few years before when she'd managed to get the attention from an art dealer.

"The last time we spoke on the phone you were just about to move into that new townhouse, and I thought you'd be needing some artwork for the walls."

Corrine pulled out a large oil canvas from behind a stack of canvases and placed it on an empty stand. Mandy recognized the scene immediately and had to draw in a deep breath to squelch the ache in her chest.

"It's beautiful, Aunt Corrine."

Her aunt smiled. "I'm glad you like it. I know how much you always enjoyed swimming in the pond up in the north pasture. Now you'll have a little piece of the Double T to keep with you in Philadelphia."

She hugged her aunt and thanked her.

Hank had retreated to the other room. She and Aunt Corrine followed the sound of his whistle to the living room where they found Hank settled in his favorite chair. The smile that had been so bright on Hank's face was gone, replaced by a weary expression. His face had turned gray and his breathing appeared labored. Panic filled her heart.

"Come sit and tell me about what you've been up to," he said.

She glanced at her aunt, who motioned her to go ahead.

"How's your job at the firm?" Hank went on.

"Fine. But I'd rather talk about you." She gathered up a deep breath of air to gain some strength. "Beau tells me you're not feeling well."

"I'm feeling just fine now that you're here."

"Don't give me that. Beau told me all about your heart condition," Mandy said, taking the lead. She was used to that in her position at the company. It was better to get it out in the open as soon as possible.

"He did, did he?"

Mandy heard Aunt Corrine's heavy sigh behind her and wondered how much they'd already argued over this very thing.

"I'm glad he told me. It seems everyone knew but me."

"It's been too long since you've been back at the Double T. I didn't want to worry you or spend the entire visit talking about me and my ticker," Hank admitted.

"Fine. Then we'll get the talking over with now and be done with it. What are you prepared to do?"

"Nothing."

*Stubborn old fool*, she fumed silently. "Then I'm sorry, Uncle Hank, but I'm not going to let it go. As far as I'm concerned, refusing surgery that will save your life is not an option."

She heard the same familiar melody she'd heard just before she and Aunt Corrine had come into the living room drifting in the room from behind her now. Since her uncle had just been struggling for air, she realized it hadn't been him whistling that sweet tune earlier, but Beau.

Beau's boot heels bouncing down the steps mixed in with the tune. He'd probably been bringing her bags to her room.

Hank lifted his eyes and stared at Beau when he walked into the living room. Beau stopped whistling as if he immediately knew by the atmosphere in the room that they were talking about Hank's condition.

"Come here, son. I'd like a word with you," Hank said. "In fact, I'd like a word with both of you."

## Chapter Three

*He was about to get burned.* Not that Beau cared much about it. If he had to do it again, he still would have told Mandy the truth about Hank's heart condition. There were too many secrets between them already.

"Don't be angry with him, Uncle Hank," Mandy said, taking Hank's hand in hers.

*What the . . . ?* She was actually defending him? Did that mean *she* wasn't angry with him anymore? Beau wondered. He could only hope. But it didn't sound like the same woman he'd just picked up at the airport.

Mandy had wasted no time at all confronting him about having the bypass surgery. By the way the tension in Hank's face seemed to ease

37

a bit, Beau realized she'd only said what she did to defuse Hank. It surely wouldn't help his heart any if his blood pressure rose through the roof.

She hadn't changed much in that way. She had a way of saying what she felt, a spirit that moved within her that seemed to guide her emotions and actions. At times she was so transparent.

Hank cast a strong eye at Beau.

"I didn't see any point in keeping the truth from her," Beau said.

"She was bound to find out sooner or later, Hank," Corrine said, placing her hand on his arm.

"I suppose," Hank conceded quietly. "It might have come better from me, though."

"It wasn't going to be good any way I got it." Mandy's eyes welled up with tears, and she blew out a quick breath. "Why are you being so stubborn about this? Beau said you could die without this surgery."

"I've got a ranch to run and as of two days ago I'm down one hand. Take me out and that makes a whole lot of work to go around for the rest of the hands."

Mandy glanced back at Beau. Her eyes were once again filled with questions and suspicion. "Is that why you asked Beau to come back?"

"If this ranch is going to run without me, I'm going to need people I can trust to work it. For your Aunt Corrine's sake," he said softly.

Corrine bunched up her fingers and closed her eyes. Mandy rose up straight in defiance. No, not defiance, fear, Beau realized. She'd been hit with too much too soon. He now knew he'd been right to warn her before they'd arrived at the ranch. It gave her time to absorb some of the shock.

"You're not going anywhere, Hank Promise," Corrine sputtered. "Not if I have anything to say about it. And you know me, I have plenty to say."

"That you do. But what happens to me, well, that's up to the good Lord, darlin'. I just figure while he's takin' his time deciding what he wants with me, I need people around me I can trust."

"You have my support in any way you need it, Uncle Hank."

Hank smiled at that, giving his face a peace Beau hadn't seen in him since he'd come back to the Double T. It was almost as if Hank was corralling everyone he loved around him. Just in time.

"I know, sweet pea."

"I'll do whatever I can to help you and Aunt Corrine until you recover from surgery."

For a brief moment the whole room stilled. Beau had hoped seeing Mandy would have changed things for Hank, would have made him see that life was definitely worth the risk of surgery. But the quick shake of Hank's head told Beau that nothing had changed.

"It's a waste of breath talking about bypass surgery."

"All the more reason why we should be talking about it, I'd think," Corrine shot back.

"Darlin', this old heart of mine is going to hold on for as long as it takes for me to get done what needs to get done. After that, it's up to the Lord," Hank said.

Corrine planted her hands on her thighs and pushed herself up to a stand, abruptly leaving the room.

The three of them stared as she retreated to her studio and quietly closed the door. No doubt there had been more than enough talk on that subject since Hank was diagnosed.

"You may be able to get away with that kind of talk with Aunt Corrine, but I'm telling you right now I won't hear any it, Uncle Hank."

"Just because it's unpleasant doesn't mean what needs to be said shouldn't be said. I need to know I can count on you."

Mandy stared at her uncle for a long moment, squashing down the foreboding feeling that filled her. Uncle Hank had always been there for her, supported her unconditionally in every way. Even when she could never live up to her father's expectations, she knew she always had Uncle Hank's support. He'd always been proud of whatever she achieved and didn't expect more. It made the sting of Damien Morgan's expectations less severe.

"Of course you have my support. Always."

He smiled his approval at her, then glanced at Beau, who had been leaning against the doorjamb from the beginning. She could tell by her uncle's reaction that he was none too pleased with Beau for spilling the beans before Hank had a chance to do it himself.

Hank stared at Beau, but he spoke to Mandy. "I want you to learn the ins and outs of running the Double T, Mandy."

Her hand flew to her chest. "You . . . you want me to work the ranch?"

"No, not actually work it. Despite being down a man, I've got enough hands to get the work done if nothin' interferes."

Mandy knew exactly what he was talking about. Some of the hands at the Double T had been with Hank since he bought the spread twenty years ago. If anything happened to Hank, it would happen to all of them. They were all family.

"I want you to learn how to run it. I need someone I can trust."

"Why me? I don't know the first thing about ranching, really. There must be a hundred cowboys within riding distance who could get the job done right—"

"But none I can trust with something so important."

She was speechless. Run the ranch? "All right. You can . . . teach me anything you think I'll need to know."

"Well, therein lies the problem. I don't have the breath in me I used to. I tire too easy. You've already seen it. I need someone else who knows ranching. Someone who still has some strength in his bones to show you everything you need to know."

She shook her head, wishing this morbidness would end and her uncle would just agree to have the surgery. If he did, he'd be back on his feet in a matter of weeks. There'd be no need for talk of numbered days and last breaths.

"Uncle Hank, don't—"

"No, sweet pea, I'm serious. That's why I want you to learn the ropes from someone else."

"Well, you can teach me what I need to know, and whatever you can't do, Aunt Corrine will do. She's been living on this ranch long enough to know how it all runs."

Hank laughed, and a twinkle lit his eye as it always did when he talked of his wife. "She's spent more time picking out the color of paints and clay to pay any attention to the way things are run around here. And that's just the way it should be. She's not a ranching woman by nature."

Hank looked at her squarely and Mandy's heart squeezed. "Mandy, darlin', I know you don't want to hear this but you have to. I'm going to die eventually and I need—"

"No! You're not going to die," she said, shoving herself to her feet. She was surprisingly steady for a woman who felt as shell-shocked as she did. "You're a young man. Too young."

"A young man with a bad ticker," he said quietly. "And I'm not messing with any doctors or surgeons who want to poke and prod me just to give me a few more months."

Tears filled her eyes again, but she remained steady, holding them back. It would do no good to break down. "So you're just going to give up? On all of us?"

Hank smiled then. She'd seen that smile before and knew the depth of his feelings for her. Instead of bringing her comfort, it made what was happening that much harder.

"I'm doing no such thing. I'm preparing for

the future. And that means teaching you all you need to know about the Double T."

"But if you're not going to teach me, then who?"

His eyes lifted to the man who was still silently standing at the far end of the living room. She followed his gaze until her own eyes settled on Beau.

"You're looking at him."

She was finding it extremely difficult to breathe. What was he thinking? What was he *doing*? Learning all the ins and outs of the Double T would require her to be in Beau's back pocket the entire time she was in Texas.

"How long can you stay?" Hank was asking in some far-away voice. *Had he really asked her to work with Beau?*

She glanced at him, pushing past the sudden panic that gripped her. His face was paler than it had been even a few minutes ago, as if the stress of this conversation alone had taken years off his life. But even with its gray color, his expression was still hopeful. This was important to him, for whatever reason, she realized. Very important. He wanted it badly enough that her mother insisted, yet again, that she drop everything and move into action.

As annoyed as she'd been with her mother's

insistence about coming to Texas, she realized this wasn't her mother talking. It was Uncle Hank, and Uncle Hank didn't demand things of her. *He asked.* How could she refuse?

"I'll work something out with Dad. I'm sure I can stay as long as you need me to. I can even work here and FedEx my work to the office. It isn't a problem."

She would make sure it wasn't a problem. Oh, her father would give her grief for being gone so long. Probably give her that standard lecture about having to pull her own weight, that he wasn't about to let anyone think he gave his daughter special privileges just because she was his daughter. If he got his gander up, she may even lose her place in the agency and have to start at the bottom again. No one would accuse Damien Morgan of nepotism.

But, it was doable, and by God, she would do it.

"You can count on me," she said resolutely.

Hank's smile shined bright through his ghostly face and told of his pleasure. Within it was also the shadow of a dying man. She didn't have that much time to convince Uncle Hank to have surgery—he was truly running out of time. And it broke her heart to see it, to think his health had deteriorated that much in the few short years since she'd seen him last.

She should have stayed in touch, she admonished herself silently. No matter what had happened between her and Beau, she shouldn't have let her relationship with her aunt and uncle suffer for it.

It was clear their reunion had taken its toll on Hank. She gave him a kiss and left him in the living room to rest. As soon as she left his side and pushed through the screen door to the front porch, anger boiled up inside her like a pot with a lid on it.

*Work side by side with Beau Gentry? Every day, every night until when?*

What was Uncle Hank thinking? Mandy fumed as she paced the wide porch. He knew about her past with Beau. He had to have thought this would be hard on her.

Maybe his health had gone so far that he wasn't thinking clearly about anything at all, let alone the surgery or what he was asking of her.

She was stunned. But not Beau. She'd seen his face while Uncle Hank made his request. And he wasn't the least bit shocked.

After Mandy paced up and down the porch a few times, Beau pushed through the screen door and stepped outside.

"You knew about this," she said, accusingly.

Beau didn't deny it.

"What, do you have a stab of guilt? Do you

figure you used me to get to my uncle all those years ago? But it didn't work. Are you back now so you can use me again to swindle the Double T out from under my uncle?"

"I won't even answer that," Beau said. His face was fierce. The hard line of his jaw told her she'd hit a nerve.

Beau stood in front of her, blocking her from pacing anymore. "Didn't you hear a thing in there? Didn't you see him? I mean really look at him?"

"Of course I did. I just can't figure out what's in this for you."

He furrowed his eyebrows. "What are you talking about?"

"You mean to tell me Hank just dreamed this up all by himself? You didn't plant this little idea in his head?"

"No," he said firmly. "You ought to know by now Hank is not a man to be swayed easily."

"He's not himself."

"He's still the same man."

She folded her arms across her chest and dropped down into the glider, forcefully rocking backward. "It seems a little convenient to me. You being here on the Double T. Hank being as sick as he is. You're in the perfect position to get what your father couldn't get himself all these years."

"You couldn't be more wrong," he said. "I'm here for one reason and one reason only. Because Hank asked me to come. He asked for my help. And whether you want to be a part of this or not doesn't concern me. You do what you have to do."

Beau arranged his straw Stetson on his head and launched himself off the porch, leaving Mandy to swing in the breeze. She watched him amble across the barnyard to the corral like she'd done hundreds of times that summer they spent together, wondering if she'd ever known Beau at all.

Maybe he was telling her the truth. Regardless of Mike Gentry's influence, Beau seemed to genuinely care about Hank. Maybe he'd come back to the Double T for the very reason he professed.

She sighed, feeling like a complete idiot for actually being disappointed that she didn't fit into the equation at all.

She *was* an idiot. Beau may be a lot of things and at one time she'd accused him of being all of them. But right now he didn't look like a man who was bent on stealing this ranch out from under a dying man. He seemed as broken-hearted as Hank.

If Hank could trust Beau, why couldn't she?

## Chapter Four

*Sleep. Who needs it?* Mandy had done without sleep so many times before that it had become a normal part of her existence to be sleep deprived.

In the earlier days of college, she'd pulled all-nighters to keep her grades up. Then later when she needed to study for finals. In more recent times, it had been because she needed to meet a strict deadline at the ad agency.

But it had been a long time since she'd been disturbed so badly by the memory of Beau Gentry that she just could not sleep. As she tossed and turned in her bed it was hard not to let the old ghost creep into the room and remind her of how much they'd loved each other. Correction, how much *she'd* loved *him*. He'd made it clear the day he'd said good-bye that he'd never really loved her.

Mandy would have thought sleep would be easy after working forty-eight hours straight on the Hill Crest Industries ad campaign. She'd allowed herself only an hour or two to sleep on the small sofa in her office after the people from Hill Crest Industries left before she hightailed to the airport to catch her flight to Texas. She should have slept like the dead.

Instead of getting much-needed sleep, she'd watched the shadows from the moonlight stretch across the room. And what sleep she had managed to catch last night in her old room on the second floor had been fitful, filled with dreams of Beau.

It wasn't the same as when he'd first left for the rodeo circuit without her. It was like something inside her had died when he left. Even as angry as she was with him for his betrayal, for saying the things he'd said, she'd mourned the loss of him. She'd missed him desperately.

The dreams she'd had last night were different. She didn't want to go there and examine what it all meant. It was better to keep her distance. She wasn't staying in Texas and neither was Beau. As soon as she succeeded in convincing Hank to have his surgery, both of them would be going back to their separate lives. And that was just fine with her.

Mandy pulled herself from the twin canopy bed she'd slept in during her youthful stays at the ranch. Corrine had kept her room exactly the same as the last time she'd been here. No wonder she was still expected to look nine years old every time she saw her aunt and uncle. The ruffled canopy bed and white dressers with gold trim looked as though they belonged to an elementary school girl. Maybe no matter how much she grew up, they'd always think of her as the little Philadelphia girl who learned to ride a pony with ease from a handful of real Texas cowboys.

She laughed with the memory as she padded to the second floor bathroom in the hallway, a pair of clean underwear and some toiletries in her hand. She knew from all her years at the Double T that you could count on most days being a simple routine that was very rarely strayed from. Breakfast was after most of the hands had already done a few hours of work. Aunt Corrine did most of the cooking in the house and prepared a picnic lunch for the men to take out on the range if that was where they were going to be that day. Many days the hands never bothered to stop for lunch at all. When they were driving the herd she'd go on ahead and set up a camp so that their meal was hot and filling when the day was done. Mandy had heard the stories, but had never been around for a real cattle drive.

Downstairs, Mandy heard voices and recognized one to be the housekeeper they'd had for years. Alice had always reminded Mandy of the housekeeper from the Brady Bunch series, except the Double T's Alice was an Apache woman who lived on the reservation not too far from the Double T.

Uncle Hank, half Apache himself, had met Alice while visiting his mother who'd lived on the reservation until she died the year after Mandy starting coming to the Double T. He'd taken Mandy to the reservation a few times for a Powwow or the Sundance Festival, and that was where she met Alice.

Alice had a daughter a few years older than Mandy. Every once in a while when she was little, Alice would bring Sara to the ranch to play with Mandy while Alice worked. She hadn't thought of Sara in years. She wondered now how her childhood friend was doing. She'd have to make a point of asking Alice when she went downstairs.

She quickly scrubbed her body clean and put on a clean pair of blue jeans she'd just purchased for the trip. They were crisp and didn't give the way her old favorite pair had when they were broken in just right. Once she began working for her father, she'd tried to develop a professional appearance, but she needed something more casual to wear around the ranch and it had been a while since she'd relaxed in casual clothes. It had been a while since she'd actually relaxed, Mandy reminded herself.

The smell of sizzling bacon and home fries drew her downstairs. In a matter of minutes she knew the bell would sound and a herd of cowpokes would come barreling through the kitchen door for breakfast. *Beau was sure to be one of them.*

After their brief argument on the porch yesterday, Beau had somehow disappeared for the rest of the afternoon. Although she had been sure she would see him at dinner last night, he hadn't shown. The empty seat in the dining room was telling not only to her but to Hank. But Hank being Hank didn't utter a word.

Beau was sure to be at breakfast this time. And most probably at every other meal. For however long she stayed at the Double T she would have to sit at the table and face him.

But there was no way around it no matter how she turned it over in her mind. And she had rolled it in every which way she could. She'd thought long and hard in those fitful hours last night, trying to find a way out of her uncle's request. The only conclusion she came to was that Hank's life was at stake and until he agreed to have the bypass surgery, she was going to placate him by working with Beau.

*Even if it killed her.*

Mandy managed to keep her scrambled eggs down during breakfast. It was easier to eat during the silence while four cowboys fed than to try to make small talk.

Beau had given her nothing more than a glance, eaten quickly, and was gone before anyone else.

An hour later she was nestled in the downstairs office, the ranch's books were scattered around her, and she was trying to make some sense of them. The thought of stealing herself away for some time without having to have Beau watching over her shoulder sounded heavenly. And since he'd been the one to disappear first, Mandy didn't have to feel guilty for avoiding him. She didn't know how she could spend the next few weeks working side by side with him every waking hour without reliving their entire relationship.

However, she wasn't having much luck sorting through records of cattle sales and receipts of feed purchases. Her luck became worse when Beau found her hideaway and knocked on the door.

"Thought I'd find you in here," he said, standing in the doorway.

She didn't reply.

"You hiding out in here, or is there something we should be working on that I don't know about?"

She fought the urge to cringe at his reference to "we."

"Thought I'd get started on some things, get acquainted with the ranch's activity by looking through the books."

"That makes for some pretty dry reading," he said, cracking an irresistible grin that she had to turn away from.

"Nothing is more dry than Statistics, and I managed to end my year with a B+ in college."

"Statistics, huh?" he said, coming into the room.

He left the door ajar and she could hear the sounds of country music from the radio in Aunt Corrine's studio. Out the window behind her, the hands were coaxing a stubborn horse from the trailer into the corral. Mitch most likely had returned with the wild horses from the auction he'd gone to earlier in the week.

"Statistics—numbers and odds, right?"

Mandy nodded.

"What do you suppose the odds would be of us being here together again?"

She glared at him. "Zero."

Beau chuckled softly and shook his head. "Then I guess you'd have to revisit your statistics books, because here we are."

"First of all, *we're* not together. Being in the same place at the same time doesn't make it so. So, even though we're physically together, that is where it ends."

He shrugged and spun his straw hat in his hand. "Maybe so. But we don't have to be enemies. You don't have to hate me."

"Hate is a strong word. That would imply that I have strong feelings for you, when I'm merely indifferent."

He spun his hat. "Do you always lie to yourself this way?"

Mandy stood up too quickly, pitching the open book in front of her to the edge of the desk and causing it to tumble to the floor. She took the extra few seconds needed to retrieve the book to compose herself.

"You're the one who left, Beau. You're the one who lied to me."

His eyes became deep and softened in a way that made her heart hammer more than her anger had. She'd almost rather Beau be smug and arrogant. It would be easier not to care about how he was feeling at that particular moment. But he was neither.

"You're right. I did lie to you eight years ago."

She sat back down and turned away from him. He didn't need to see how much his betrayal still affected her.

"But not in the way you think. I lied when I told you I didn't love you." The deep timbre of his voice was smooth, filled with emotion.

Mandy shrunk back in her seat, her body trembling. What was he saying?

"After all this time I'm supposed to believe that?"

"Yes." He shrugged and sighed heavily, taking a few steps closer to the desk. Much too close. "Well. Maybe not. But you don't have to take my word for it. Just think of us. If you let yourself think back to what we were like when we were together, you'll remember that what we shared was real. No man can fake that kind of emotion, Mandy."

"You did."

He shook his head. "If eight years of living with my lie has brought you to hating me this much, well then I guess I deserve it. It was wrong of me to take the easy way out."

Mandy lifted her chin. "Is this your way of apologizing?"

"Would you accept it?"

"No."

"Well, it's an apology regardless. One that is long overdue."

"What about Hank?"

"What about him?"

She laughed sardonically.

"I told you Hank doesn't harbor any ill feelings for me. That's why I'm here."

They stared at each other for a long moment. Did he really expect her to forgive him? For everything? Part of her wanted to forgive him, and that made what she was feeling much worse.

"What do you want from me, Beau?" she asked softly.

For a fraction of a second he looked hurt. The lines around his eyes shadowed and his jaw tightened.

"Nothing."

He cleared his throat, dragged his gaze from her, and headed toward the door.

Mandy hadn't realized she was breathing much too heavily until it looked as though he was going to leave without turning back. And then he did turn back and her heart skipped a beat.

"If you are really interested in learning about the ranch, a good way to do it is to get your nose out of those books and come with me."

He walked through the door and Mandy called out to him, "Where are you going?"

He appeared in the doorway again and placed his hands high on the doorjamb on both sides of the door, filling the space completely. *Locking her in.*

"For a start, to meet with the cattle auctioneer. Then some of the other people in the area who work with the ranch on a yearly basis to keep things running smooth. You'll find all their names and numbers in those books you've been poring over. But until you meet them face to face and see how they operate, you won't really have a handle on how things are done. You with me?"

She didn't answer. She didn't want to do this. She didn't want to be with Beau. But she had to. She closed the book in front of her and placed it back in its rightful place before grabbing her hat.

*You're doing this for Hank*, Beau kept reminding himself. Still, he couldn't help but think that part of this was for him, too. A second chance of sorts to go back and do it right, make amends for the wrong he'd done to Mandy.

Mandy didn't believe him when he'd told her he'd lied about not loving her. And why would she? She'd had eight long years of hearing those awful words in her head, reliving the pain she had felt when he'd rejected her. And she still felt it. Every time she glanced his way, he could see the pain in those rich brown eyes of hers. He hated himself for it.

And he felt the pain, too. If he could go back, he would erase that pained expression from her face. Kiss her sweet lips and. . . .

No. He couldn't go back. And even if he could, he realized now that it wouldn't have changed anything. The only thing he could hope for now was to move forward.

After hearing John Bower from the feed store go on and on about this and that and nothing at all, they were back in the truck heading back to the Double T. Mandy had been talkative with the feed store owner, but now that they were alone, she was quiet again.

Unable to take the sound of tires eating up the highway, Beau turned on the radio. Within minutes of looking at the familiar Texas farmland on both sides of the road, tension eased from his muscles.

Mandy leaned forward and turned off the radio.

"What'd you do that for?"

Glaring at him, she said, "You're whistling out of tune again."

Then she turned away to look out her window, but not quick enough for him to miss the smile she was trying to hide from him. A real honest-to-goodness smile. Lord have mercy, they were finally making progress!

He couldn't keep his lips from stretching into a satisfied grin. "Admit it, you like it when I whistle."

"Do not."

"Yeah, you do."

"In your dreams."

He could hear her soft chuckle even with her face turned toward the open window, the wind blowing her blond streaks in a wild mess around her face.

She finally looked at him and he caught a first real look at her smile. Lord, how he'd missed that face.

"Okay, you win. I think it's kind of funny."

He pretended to be offended. "What's wrong with the way I whistle? It's jovial, it's—"

"Off-key! You can't carry a tune to save your life," she said, laughing. "And what's worse is you think you're on-key, so you whistle louder.

Then you tap your other foot on the floorboard to give it added emphasis. Drives me crazy."

He laughed himself, taking his eyes off the road a time or two to enjoy her laughter.

"And it doesn't matter where you are in the house or in the barnyard, I know where you are because I hear you whistling all over the entire ranch."

"You keeping tabs on me again?"

Her expression changed. Afraid to break this sudden connection between them, he quickly changed the subject.

"So what have you been doing these last eight years?"

She adjusted herself in the seat before she spoke. "If you're looking for a complete run-down of my life it could take all day."

"Give me the *Reader's Digest* version." In truth, Beau would have taken all day to hear about all he'd missed in Mandy's life. But he knew as soon as they got back to the ranch, there'd be other people to intrude on the solitude he had with Mandy now. Selfish as it was, he liked having her all to himself. One of the unexpected little perks of Hank's plan.

"Hmm. I lived in Boston for a few years while attending college, and now I work for my father's advertising firm."

"Just like you always planned."

"Yeah," she said quietly.

"I imagine advertising must be a high-stress job. Demanding. How'd you manage to get away for a few weeks like this on such short notice?"

She laughed again and he felt his heart skip a beat. It had been a long time since he'd heard that musical lilt in her voice. Forgotten how much it reeled him in.

The distance between them was so great. But was it insurmountable? Beau didn't want to think so.

"I don't sleep much."

"Can't live on no sleep. I guess it's good you're getting away for while then. At least for the rest."

"Guess again. I probably won't be sleeping much while I'm here, either. I had a big ad campaign presentation due right before I flew out. I worked two days straight on it. That's why I looked like I'd survived a tornado when you picked me up at the airport."

"You mean, that wasn't the latest style coming out of all those New York City boutiques this year?"

"Hardly. After the Hill Crest Industries people left I managed to catch a few hours of sleep on the sofa in my office right before I took my flight to Texas. I thought I'd nailed that presentation. But Dad . . ."

She stopped herself from saying anything more. And she didn't really have to. This had been a bone of contention between Mandy and Damien Morgan all her life. Nothing Mandy managed to achieve was ever quite good enough to live up to her father's expectations.

That was something Beau and Mandy always had in common, a common thread that bound them. Unlike Mandy, who forged ahead, trying to do her best to win that elusive approval, Beau had accepted early on that the life Mike Gentry thought Beau should be living wasn't in line with what Beau wanted for himself.

"Anyway, the Hill Crest Industries people haven't made a decision yet. Just in case they aren't quite as happy with the work I've presented and want a different slant, I'll be burning the midnight oil to produce something new."

"You've got to sleep sometime."

"Yeah, well, sleep is overrated."

He stared at her. The road ahead was flat and straight and he didn't mind taking the extra few seconds to linger on her mouth to see her smile had faded.

"Are you happy?" *Please tell me you are,* Beau prayed silently. He wanted to hear that the life he'd sent her back to was the life she wanted and now loved. He needed to know that giving her up eight years ago hadn't been in vain.

"What about you?" she said, turning his question back to him. "You're going for World Champion this year, right?"

"Yeah," he said quietly. Yes, he was. As soon as he knew Hank was going to be okay, he'd hightail it back to the circuit. The World Championship title was within his reach for the first time in his career, and there was no way he was going to miss it.

"Doesn't this time away put a cramp in things?"

"A little," he said honestly. By rights he should be busting his butt, hitting every rodeo he could to make sure his spot was secure. He'd told Hank he might steal himself away from the ranch for one of the closer shows coming up. Mitch being gone put a dent in that plan, but now that Mitch was back there was no reason he couldn't.

"Then I guess it's in both our best interests to convince Hank to have that surgery as soon as possible. So we can both get back to our lives."

"Yeah."

He didn't know why, but the thought of leaving Texas didn't seem so bad. Leaving Texas without Mandy didn't sit as well with him. He'd done it before. He was going to do it again. He had a feeling it wasn't going to be any easier the second time around.

## Chapter Five

Mandy ran a soft cloth over the pictures on the fireplace mantel, giving herself a good long stare at each one before dropping them back into place.

"Now what do you think you're doing," Alice said, coming into the wide pine-paneled room carrying a bucket and scrubs. "Your aunt and uncle hired me for a reason, young lady. You'll be doing no housecleaning while I'm still walking around these floors."

"I was looking at the picture and got my fingerprints all over the glass. I made the mess, I figured I might as well be the one to clean it up. Besides, it gave me a reason to linger a little longer."

"If you do it all, I'll have nothing left to do."

Mandy chuckled softly. "I'm sure these hands track in enough dirt and muck to keep you busy."

"That they do," Alice said, smiling.

She dropped the bucket on the floor and stood next to Mandy by the mantel.

"Every so often Corrine would rifle through that big box of photos and rearrange the pictures on the mantel. As soon as she knew you were coming she did it again. We're all so happy having you back with us."

Squashing a cascade of guilt, Mandy picked up a picture and showed it to Alice. "Remember this one?"

Alice's face grew solemn. "That I do."

It was the first time she'd visited the reservation with Uncle Hank and Aunt Corrine, her first summer at the Double T.

Alice and her daughter, Sara, lived on the reservation. Aunt Corrine had told her all about Sara when her mother had gone home to Philadelphia, leaving Mandy behind for the first time. She'd been so sad that first week that everyone, including Alice, thought it would do Mandy a world of good to visit and have the two young girls play together while Hank visited with his mother.

"That snapshot was taken the day you met my Sara," Alice said, taking the photo from her.

"How is Sara doing?"

"Like you, she hasn't been home in a while. In fact, she hasn't been back home since that summer before you left."

"That's too bad. I was hoping to see her."

Alice's face brightened. "I have her address in California. I'm sure she'd love it if you dropped her a line now and then. Even though she doesn't say it, I think she's homesick for Texas."

"I'd like that. Sometimes you don't know just how homesick you are until you come home."

"Ain't that the truth."

Mandy placed the picture down carefully on the mantel.

"It's so good to have you back home," Alice said, picking up her bucket and brushes again.

She left Mandy alone to look at the pictures. Mandy heard the high-pitched whinny of a pony out in the corral filtering in from the open window. There was a slight breeze today, but she knew it would do little to lessen the effects of the hot sun.

As she made her way down the row of pictures, her hand stopped on an old photograph. It was taken the same day Mandy had met Sara on the reservation. Her uncle had looked so handsome when he was a young man. She'd forgotten just how handsome. She remembered sitting on his lap as Aunt Corrine snapped the shot of them with Hank's mother.

Mandy had only met Regina Promise the one time. She remembered her as being very old, but very kind, like Hank. Looking at the picture now, she didn't seem that old at all. Worn perhaps, from a hard life, but beautiful with her thick dark hair and eyes. She stared at the picture for a long time until she heard the sound of whistling in the barnyard.

*Beau.*

Sighing, she dropped the picture back in place, and took the next one, immediately wishing she hadn't. Why on earth would Aunt Corrine keep this picture?

Deep longing swept through her as she stared down at a young Beau Gentry sitting on the porch steps. His arm was lazily draped around Mandy's shoulders. She stared up at him like the star-crossed, lovesick teenager she was. Her hair was pulled back in a tight ponytail, making her look even younger. She was wearing a pair of faded shorts that were too tight, but she had liked the way Beau's eyes lit up when he saw her in them.

Uncle Hank, on the other hand, did nothing but scowl when she wore them. She couldn't

help but laugh at the memory. At every opportunity he'd tell her there was enough testoster-
one running wild on the ranch. She didn't have
to give the hands any more reason to make fools
of themselves.

But not Beau. Oh, he'd made a fool of himself, all right. But she never cared. He'd tell her
over and over again that she was the prettiest
thing his eyes had ever seen.

And like the fool she was, she had believed
him.

"Now ain't she the prettiest thing you ever
did see?" Beau said, leaning the full weight of
his body against the fence.

"Nothing more beautiful," Hank agreed.

And she was, Beau thought with awe.
Though he could certainly think of at least one
other filly who'd spun his head by her sheer
beauty.

"Be careful. This little girl's a spitfire," Hank
warned. "Gotta handle her with kid gloves.
Even then I think she'd just as soon stomp you
in the ground just for looking at her."

"That's the way I love 'em," Beau said, se-
curing his hat firmly on his head as he opened
the gate to the corral. "The feistier the better.
Makes it all worth it in the end."

"You going to test her out?"

"If she'll have me."

Hank nodded knowingly. "Lady like this needs to be taken real slow," he said. "You can't tie her down or try to make her think you're the one in control. She won't give up before she's ready."

The screen door slammed hard and Beau turned to see Mandy standing on the porch, peering out at them by the corral. She stood on the top step, her hands slipped deep into the pockets of her crisp denim blues.

"I've been down this road before," Beau assured his old friend. "I think I can handle myself."

Chuckling, Hank cast a quick glance at the porch, then back at Beau. "We are talking about the horse now, aren't we, son?"

Beau shoved his hat low on his head and chuckled. " 'Course."

He watched Mandy out of the corner of his eye as she strode through the yard toward the corral. He shouldn't be nervous. He'd done this a thousand times over, but suddenly it was if he'd been transported back to the first time he'd climbed into a shoot to mount.

When he finished rosining up his rigging, he pulled on his leather gloves and strode into the shoot, where he could see the young filly was already itching to charge out bucking.

The wild horses Mitch had just purchased at auction were both mares, and they were still testing their new boundaries. It would take a while for Mitch to do his magic and gentle them enough to be good riding horses. Still, Beau couldn't help but take a chance at trying to mount one of them when their spirit was still raw and free, and feel that adrenaline rush when in her wild way she tried to buck him off. It had been over a month since his last rodeo, and every nerve ending in him was itching to get back to riding again.

He fought the urge to steal another quick glance at Mandy, to see if she was hanging on the fence of the corral, chewing on her lip with anticipation like she used to do, or if she was hiding her eyes for fear of what was to come. The very first rodeo he'd ever entered, she was there standing at the gate just the way she was now. Except then, he'd been so distracted by that kiss for luck she'd given him, he'd been thrown from his mount just as soon as he left the shoot. He'd crawled out of the arena like a beat dog with his tail tucked between his legs.

Mandy had a way of making him feel he could do anything back then. He'd been so green, but not to Mandy. She'd just looked at him, her breaths kind of shallow like she'd had the air sucked from her lungs instead of him when he hit the dusty ground. She'd said, "Come on, Beau, there's another rodeo this afternoon."

That was all. Not a word said about being bucked off, not a mention of what had happened, as if it didn't matter. A little shove from behind to move him in the right direction and Mandy had him feeling like he could move a mountain. He'd forgotten that about her. But he remembered now. To Mandy, falling really didn't matter.

It mattered a whole lot to him, though. When he wanted to find the nearest hole to crawl into, she just dusted herself off and forged ahead.

He could see she applied the same principle to her own life. Instead of accepting that she'd never be exactly what her old man wanted of her, she tried anyway. And she had gotten far through trying. Mandy had told him years ago that Damien Morgan didn't give free rides. Daughter or no daughter, if she didn't pull her weight at his advertising firm, she wouldn't be there. He had the feeling she pulled her weight and a whole lot more to get where she was today.

Beau had always admired that about her. She didn't give up when she wanted something badly. And neither did he. He'd gone on the rodeo circuit wet behind the ears and practically penniless. After every fall, every ride, he recalled Hank's strength and applied it to his ride until he was scoring. And even though he'd left her behind, he held on to Mandy's belief that he could do it, he could win. After every spill, every disappointed end of the day, he felt her gentle nudge from behind to keep going strong. Now he was one of the best on the circuit, and the World Championship title could be his.

This mare wanted no part of him as he approached the shoot. And why would she? Not too long ago she'd had no barriers keeping her from running free. Now it didn't matter how much room she had, she was caged like a bird who'd once soared the skies.

When she'd settled some, Beau talked soothingly to her. He got close enough to let her get the scent of him, let her take her time and get her fill while he saddled her good and tight. The tighter the better. All the while talking as he eased himself into position so he could mount her.

"You sure you want to do this?" Mitch asked, ready at the gate.

Beau stared at a spot on the mare's neck, felt anticipation surge through his veins, and nodded once. It always happens in a heartbeat after that. The young mare sees her shot at freedom again when the gate flies opens, explodes out into the corral, and realizes she still has company.

Beau held on, dug his boot heels into her side and rode for all it was worth. He'd missed it. Four long weeks of not riding. He lasted until he thought the mare had had enough and he jumped off and raced out of her way.

Still feeling the adrenaline high from his ride, he glanced at the spot where Mandy stood next to Hank. She was standing on the rail of the corral, hanging on with a tight grip as if her life depended on it. And she was smiling with a face filled with pride. Mercy, it was like he'd ridden just for her instead of himself. And maybe he had.

He pulled off his hat and smacked it on his chaps, creating a small dust cloud as he walked toward the fence, shaking his head as he went. He was such an idiot. Had he really been trying to impress Mandy, show her that like she had, he'd risen above and achieved what he'd set out to do?

Hank was looking more worn for the wear when Beau reached them. Being in the hot sun had to take a lot out of him. He'd slowed down considerably since his diagnosis, trying to reserve his energy, but Hank wasn't a man who could be contained for too long. No doubt he'd been up and at it with the rest of the hands this morning and was now feeling the ill effects of overdoing it.

"I'd forgotten what it was like to see you ride," Mandy said. Her smile was gone. Now she shook her head slightly, her delicate lips twisting into a frown.

"She wasn't all that uptight about me being there."

"Bunch of fool cowboys, every single bow-legged one of you," Mandy replied.

"You didn't always think that way, doll," Hank said, chuckling as he turned and slowly headed back to the house.

Watching her uncle go, Mandy said, "I was young and foolish myself back then."

Beau dropped his hat low on his head to shield the sun so he could stare at her. Lord, but this woman was beautiful out here in the sunshine. "Got to have something to believe in."

She eyed him squarely. "I've never been a good judge of character."

Beau couldn't help but laugh. "Admit it. You like to see me ride."

"What makes you so sure?"

"I saw you riding the fence. Saw you smiling, too. You still like watching me."

"It's hot as Hades out here. I came out to make sure Hank wasn't overdoing it."

"If that were true you'd have followed him back in the house when he left. Since you're still here, I can only guess you came out to see me."

Rolling her eyes, she sputtered, "In your dreams."

"All my dreams are about you, Mandy."

And *that* was definitely the wrong thing to say.

## Chapter Six

She needed to laugh more, Beau decided.

Mandy may not have realized it yet. She may have even forgotten what it was like to *be* happy. But Beau was going to make it his mission to remind her. He was going to do all he could to make her laugh again.

Except for that brief time in the truck when she'd giggled at his whistling, Mandy had been stingy with her laughter. Somewhere buried behind all the deadlines and late nights of work was the same girl who had thrown his heart for a loop eight years ago.

It was only right that she'd be on edge about Hank. They all were. But Beau had the feeling that Mandy had lost the ability to just laugh at life. It couldn't be that she was still angry with him. It was more than that. She wasn't *happy* anymore. Not like she used to be anyway. Before he left the Double T again he was going to make sure she was happy once more.

He found Mandy nestled on the porch glider, staring off into the horizon as if she were deep in thought. It was late morning and the sun was already brutally beating down on them. As he approached the porch, he saw a half-full glass of lemonade in her hand. One leg was tucked under the other, showing off inches of creamy skin her denim shorts couldn't hide.

As his boots hit the bottom porch step, she snapped her gaze toward him and heaved a slow sigh.

Knowing he disturbed her, but not letting it sway him, he forged on. "Where's Hank?"

"It's too hot. He and Aunt Corrine are taking a nap in the air conditioning."

"This early, huh? It's scarcely mid-morning."

"Yeah," was all she said in a low voice, as she shifted her gaze back to the horizon.

Hank frequently took naps in the afternoon, something he'd never done when Beau had known him years ago. The thick heat made it hard for him to catch his breath. Better for him to stay inside. Which is why it surprised him to find Mandy outside as well, if she didn't have to be. She wasn't yet used to the Texas sun.

"You look like you could use some cooling off," he said.

Mandy glared at him.

Smiling sheepishly, he amended his remark. "I didn't mean it the way it sounded."

"If you say so."

"The wind's not moving at all today, not that it ever does. You might be more comfortable yourself if you stayed out of the heat, is all I was saying."

She hesitated a minute. "I like looking at the ranch. It's been a long time since I've just let myself sit and enjoy the scenery."

He wanted to sit next to her on the glider, but knew Mandy probably wouldn't welcome him there. He remained in place at the edge of the porch and pulled off his hat, looking out over the ranch in the same direction Mandy was looking.

It was truly beautiful. It was a sight he'd committed to memory and longed for on many occasions when the road ahead was too long with too many towns in between. There was something about coming home. And even though the Double T had never been his home, Beau had longed for the feelings it evoked when yearning for home set in.

"Things aren't as fast down here as they must be up in Philadelphia. I imagine advertising must be a fairly wild ride."

She nodded her head, tossing him a wry grin. He squashed the familiar zing that always took hold of him when he saw Mandy's smile.

"Feels good to catch my breath, though," she said.

"I have plenty of time for catching my breath after my butt hits the hard ground."

She glanced at him quickly, her eyebrows crinkling into an adorable frown, then gave a weak smile at his attempt at a joke.

She was keeping herself in check, he realized. Holding back any kind of emotional response to keep from opening up to him. She had a lot on her mind, not the least of which was Hank. Drawing a deep breath of hot Texas air, he forged ahead, giving it another try.

"The way I see it, we have two choices."

"And what would they be?"

"The cabin in the hills needs to be stocked with supplies. One of the hands is going to spend some time up there before the cattle roundup. We can either spend the afternoon getting all that squared away. . . ."

"Or?"

"Give ourselves a much-needed break and

head up to the creek where that old rope swing used to be. It's going to be a hot afternoon."

"Texas in August, Beau. Every afternoon is hot."

"Well, it's going to be even more so. I think it's high time we turned our attention away from ranch business and took a swim."

The flash of pain that crossed her face was instantaneous. She was quick, averting her gaze to look down at the book in her lap, but Beau saw enough to know that memories of the two of them were still very fresh in her mind. He'd had enough memories of his own float to the surface during the last month.

"If you have your heart set on going for a swim, then go for it. I'll just have to pass."

"Forget how to swim?"

"Forgot my bathing suit."

His lips stretched into a wicked grin. "That isn't a problem with me."

"Well it is for me." She tried to sound annoyed, glaring at him as if she were about to slap him. But she couldn't fool him. A smile was sitting just beneath the surface. Being Mandy, though, she was too stubborn to show it.

He'd work on that. He liked a challenge. And Mandy was about as pretty a challenge as a man could encounter.

"Then I guess stocking the cabin wins out."

Her shoulders slumped slightly. "I'm really not up to it, Beau. Can't one of the other hands get the cabin set? Riding up to the hills will take all day."

"Which is why no one else can go. The hands have got other duties around here."

"I don't want to be gone all that long."

"You know Corrine. She'll make sure Hank rests if she has to hog-tie him."

That remark was rewarded with a smile. It always amazed him how strong his heart beat in his chest with one flash of a smile from Mandy Morgan.

"She would, too," Mandy said, giving a soft giggle.

"It doesn't make sense to hang around and wait for something to happen. Hank's going to be fine."

If he had his way, everything would be fine for Mandy, too. Despite the tension surrounding their reasons for coming to Texas, Beau could see how much more relaxed Mandy was after being at the ranch for a few days. She'd all but stopped checking her watch every fifteen minutes.

When he came up on her as she sat on the glider, it was immediately apparent that some of the stress that had tightened her features had eased, smoothing out the lines of worry. Oh, she was still worried about her uncle, but it was different. There wasn't a fast-paced urgency about her anymore. Just taking the time to enjoy the beauty of the horizon was a huge improvement over the nervous energy that had her wearing a path back and forth on the living room rug.

Still, he could tell she hadn't left all those worries behind. Half her mind was still in Philadelphia and half was here in Texas worrying about Hank.

"I don't know," she said.

"I do. Get your hat."

He turned and strode off the porch, propping his cowboy hat on his head as he moved, before she could utter a word of protest.

She shouldn't have come. Even as she slid into the passenger seat of Beau's truck, Mandy was second-guessing her decision to join him.

But even as her mind waged war with her decision, she had to admit Beau was right. She couldn't wile away the hours hoping Hank would change his mind about surgery. She'd only drive herself and everyone else crazy with nervous energy.

Sitting on the porch, even with her worrying, had done her some good. For the first time in a long time she felt her tension ease and her muscles unwind. She loved the Double T, loved visiting with her aunt and uncle. She loved being in Texas, despite the memories that had kept her away all these years. She'd have to make sure she didn't let another eight years go by without visiting.

She had to admit, too—at least a little part of her wanted to be with Beau. Even that little admission set her off-kilter.

"The cattle drive is the one thing I always missed every summer when I went home," Mandy said, helping to load the last of the supplies they'd just purchased into the back of the truck.

Beau adjusted his straw hat to shield the sun so he could look at her. "That's right, you always had to go back home for school before the cattle were brought in every year."

She nodded, recalling the disappointment she had always felt when she had to leave. "I used to beg Uncle Hank to convince Mom to let me stay just until then. I figured all those riding lessons ought to be put to good use out here on the ranch."

She shook her head as she climbed into the truck and slammed the door. She waited for Beau to gun the engine before she continued.

"Mom would have no part of it. I think she

was afraid I'd change my mind all together and not want to come home at all."

"Did you want that?"

Mandy lifted her shoulder in an idle shrug. "Sometimes. Aunt Corrine used to paint such wonderful stories about the cattle drive. She's not your typical rancher's wife. I always figured for her to want to go, it had to be a good time, despite the work."

"There's always a first time. You don't need your mom's permission anymore. You could do it this year. I'm sure Hank would welcome the helping hand."

"Unless the drive is in a few weeks, I won't be here this year either."

"You planning on leaving soon?"

She sighed and brushed away the tendrils of hair from around her face. "I don't want to. But I can't hang around here forever hoping I can convince Hank to have surgery."

"Hank doesn't have forever. Any luck?"

"Every time I bring up the subject, he puts me off. He doesn't want to talk about it. Then Aunt Corrine gets upset and leaves the room. They're beginning to look an awful lot like my parents did when I was a kid."

They were both quiet a moment. The sound of the wheels running over dry pavement ate into the silence.

"I was hoping. . . ." Beau started. He didn't have to finish. It echoed her exact feelings on the subject.

*Hank.* What was she going to do about him? He *didn't* have forever to make up his mind about surgery. In the few days she'd been at the Double T she'd seen how much his condition had deteriorated. Just being out in the hot sun this morning had beaten him to the ground.

Ever since she could remember, Hank had loved rodeo and ranching. When she was young, she'd seen him in a few rodeos. He'd been off the road for years, but he still entered a few now and then. There was a spark that ignited to a flame in each of those cowboys who entered the shoot to mount their bronc. She'd seen it in Hank many times when he was talking of rodeo or getting ready for a ride.

And she'd seen it in Beau that morning. He loved to ride. Part of her loved to watch him ride, too. Although for the last eight years she hadn't been to a single rodeo, the sudden rush of adrenaline that used to hit her when the shoot opened quickly came charging back. Her heart pounded so hard in her chest she thought it would explode.

She knew she should have followed Hank back into the house. Instead, it was as though she were transformed back to sixteen. She caught the twinkle of pride in Beau's dark eyes and it took her breath away. As it always did.

*All my dreams are about you, Mandy.*

Why on earth did he have to say that? She didn't believe a word of it, of course. Beau had always flirted with her. He had enough cowboy charm to fill the quota for the state of Texas.

She recalled how she'd spun on her heels and charged back to the house with her fists balled merely to hide the fact that she'd actually been flattered by his words. They'd been stupid words said at the exact right time and her heart actually did a flip. She was half afraid she'd humiliate herself further by adding a girlish sigh to it, and knew she needed to put some distance between herself and Beau.

And now she was alone with him again.

"I saw you on that mare this morning," she said. "Aren't you itching to get back on the road, too?"

"It can wait a while."

She stared at him for a moment, watching his profile as his eyes remained on the road ahead.

*Dreams.* She hadn't been Beau's dream.

"You always said you wanted to rodeo."

"Yeah."

"And no regrets?"

"Just you."

*Foolish, foolish, foolish.* She'd walked right

into that one and still she couldn't believe she'd done it. What was she fishing for anyway? Some admission that part of what Beau had said was actually true?

"I find it hard to believe mine was the only heart you ever broke, Beau Gentry."

He lifted a shoulder in a lazy shrug. "I wouldn't know."

"Really? No one special girl who made you turn your head before climbing into the shoot?"

He turned to her then, flashing her a smile that seemed completely sexy and sincere all at the same time. *She hated when he did that.* "You're the only woman who ever made my head spin, Mandy."

She sputtered.

Beau chuckled, and it made her all the more irritated.

"I'm never anyplace long enough for something special. Who knows, maybe there were a few broken hearts along the way, but not because of promises I made. Most girls I meet on the circuit know the life of a rodeo cowboy. Nothing lasts that long."

Annoyance rose up inside her like bile at the thought of Beau with another woman. Of course there'd been other girls for Beau. There had to have been. He was young and handsome and strong. He was the perfect cowboy who every woman dreamed of. Even she'd dated other men during the eight years that separated them. Still, she turned away from his probing gaze to hide the stab of jealousy chipping away at her.

"I told my tale, now fess up. What about you?"

"What about me?" she asked, still averting her gaze.

"Any one man in your life make you think of white picket fences and puppy dogs and kids in the backyard?"

"A few."

She felt more than heard his hesitation, as if it were something tangible. "A few, huh? Special ones or just . . . guys you knew?"

Forcing her voice to sound nonchalant, she replied, "There were a few guys that were special."

Mandy turned her attention away from the scenery to glance at Beau. She didn't want him to think she'd spent the last years pining over him. But in truth—a truth she'd only recently realized—she had.

Beau was brooding. That much was clear. One arm was slung heavy over the steering wheel while the other was draped across the open window. There was a sudden droopiness in his shoulders, as if she'd deflated his spirit in some way. *Probably his ego,* she thought wryly.

She shouldn't like that mentioning an old boyfriend could turn him a little green, but she did. As green as she'd been. She'd have to work on that. She didn't want to be feeling anything at all for Beau Gentry.

There was a brief silence that made Mandy think talk of old flames had killed the conversation completely. It was just as well. She'd only end up admitting to him that although she'd had many dates, even long-term boyfriends, since she'd been with Beau, they didn't stand a chance. None of them made her feel as special and cherished as Beau had.

"They didn't have staying power," she finally admitted quietly.

Beau nodded, but didn't look at her.

The asphalt disappeared beneath them and turned to dirt as they made their way up the narrow mountain road to the cabin. The truck bounced and bobbed as the tires hit the small ruts in the road left over from a heavy downpour earlier in the season.

After a few more minutes of strained silence, Beau glanced at the clouds and said, "Looks like a storm might be blowing in. We should get these things unloaded at the cabin before it starts."

Mandy glanced up at the sky. "The truck has four-wheel drive though, doesn't it?"

"Yeah, but the ground is so dry this time of the year it's going to sop up any moisture it can. If the rain is bad enough, the creek will rise over its banks and wash out the road. Might turn into a mud bog before long."

"How far is the cabin?"

"Not too far. Did you carry that cell phone of yours with you?"

She thought back to the last time she'd had her cell phone. It was at the airport when she'd first arrived. She recalled her frustration over not being able to use it to call for another ride. Normally her link to her job and her life, it seemed strange that she hadn't even picked it up since.

"Ah, no, I haven't even charged it since I arrived. Why?"

The worried look on Beau's face made her stomach drop.

He just shrugged.

"My truck doesn't have a radio in it like Mitch and George's do. I didn't think much about it until we hit the dirt road. If it does wash out and we have to turn back to the cabin overnight, it'd be nice to be able to contact the ranch and let them know."

Overnight? With Beau? No, that definitely couldn't happen.

"We should probably turn back now then," Mandy said.

"It'd be a waste of time. We've got everything in the back. It'll get soaked if we get caught in a downpour. Better off unloading at the cabin. We'll be back soon enough."

"But if we get stuck. . . ." She let her words run off, unable to say them aloud. What would they do if they were stuck together in inescapably small quarters? If her memory served her correctly, the cabin was nothing more than one room with a potbelly stove, a handful of bunks, and a small card table. Much too small for her to spend any length of time alone with Beau.

He had taken her there once long ago. Mandy knew she shouldn't be there alone with Beau, not with the way they were feeling about each other. It was too easy, too tempting to give in to their feelings. They were both too young.

They hadn't stayed long. Beau knew Uncle Hank would have shot him if they'd been caught together. Beau held a deep respect for her uncle, or so she'd thought at the time. He'd said he'd respected her too much to. At the time, it had made her feel incredibly special and loved, despite the adolescent longings she had to be with Beau.

But she wasn't an adolescent anymore. And no matter how hard she tried to tell herself that she was over Beau Gentry, it was becoming increasingly hard to keep lying to herself. She wasn't over him at all. And being trapped alone with him would only bring that realization crashing down upon her like a tidal wave.

## Chapter Seven

Less than fifteen minutes later, the truck pulled up in front of a small one-room cabin in the high country. It had been quite a feat for Beau to navigate the dirt road, given the fact it had been washed out in places and gouged with ruts from past storms. But they'd managed to make it, thanks to four-wheel drive.

Mandy stepped out of the cab of the truck and looked at the rolling gray sky. It was black with clouds that hung low and ominous, and it was getting darker still. Every so often the entire sky would flash with a zing of lightning and be chased by a rumble or crack of thunder. The torrential downpour hadn't come yet, but the light drizzle that had started promised it was just on their heels.

Most all the supplies were tucked underneath a tarp in the back of the truck. They left everything in the truck and went inside.

Beau wasted no time at all in lighting a gas lamp set on a small table in the center of the room. The light cast an amber glow around the room. Mandy hugged herself to keep the chill of the cabin from making her shiver. It didn't work. Wet clothes and a cold cabin didn't make for warmth.

She pushed past the thought that only being in the warmth of Beau's arms would chase away the chill.

"We'll drop everything inside first and unload it later."

She looked around the compact cabin. It was only meant for a few cowboys while the herd was in the high country. Certainly not meant for a romantic interlude.

The sturdy wood table sitting in the center of the room was about all the furniture the small cabin had. A small kettle woodstove stood at one end of the room, while on the opposite side four bunks were built into the wall. They were clear of bedding, just clean, bare mattresses.

She needed to get out of there. Following

Beau outside she saw that it had started to rain. That was good and bad. They needed to work fast to unload the truck so they could head back. But it was good because the rain made her work harder and it was better to put this anxious energy into physical effort rather than allowing her mind wander to thoughts of Beau.

The clouds were practically sitting on their shoulders as they unloaded box after box of supplies that the hands would need for the cattle drive. Halfway through unloading the sky opened up and swallowed them in a downpour.

Beau yanked two bright yellow rain slickers from the rack in the cabin and handed Mandy one.

"We have to hurry or we'll never make it back."

Beau didn't need to say more than that. There was no way Mandy was going to get caught alone with Beau until weather cleared and the road dried. Her aunt and uncle would worry, regardless of the fact that she was now an adult, quite capable of living on her own.

Once they were done, and completely out of breath from running back and forth from the truck to the cabin, they settled in the cabin and pulled off their wet slickers.

Beau shook out the slickers and hung them near the stove to dry while he watched Mandy.

"I hope this rain cools off the air," Mandy said, pulling off her straw hat and fingering the wet ends of her hair. She pulled out the comb she'd secured earlier in the back of her head and used it to free the snarls caused by the wind and choking humidity.

"It'll probably sizzle as it hits the ground. Won't do much if we don't have any breeze."

"Should we chance unpacking everything, or just head back before the road washes out?"

"You in a hurry?" he said.

"Aren't you?"

Beau didn't answer. What on earth could he say? The thought of being stranded in the cabin with Mandy was just too tempting. He thought about the dirt road down by the creek and knew they were taking their chances staying too long. It was only a matter of time before the creek jumped its banks and flowed over the road. There'd be no passing it by truck. The only way they'd be able to get back to the ranch was by horse. And since they didn't take any, they'd be stuck.

He had to admit he'd give anything to just spend some time alone with Mandy, to try to capture some of that magic he'd been feeling between them. But his conscience getting the better of him, he conceded. "You're right. We'd best be getting out of here. We can leave this for another day when the weather is on our side."

She was fiddling with her hair with some pearly comb she'd had hidden under her straw cowboy hat. As soon as she was finished brushing out the ends with it, she'd twirled her hair into some kind of twist and secured it with the comb.

He was finding it difficult to breathe. Not that it was any surprise to Beau. Mandy had always had a way of catching him off-guard, making his mouth go dry for wanting her. It had been a long time since he'd been caught in the tidal wave of feelings that he'd held for Mandy alone.

She'd had some special loves, she'd said on the ride up. Beau had always thought there might be someone special, had hoped that she'd been happy. He just didn't think it'd feel so much like a kick in the gut to know about it. He'd wanted her to be happy with him, kissing him in his arms like she used to do. He wanted to think that the smile she shined up at him in the moonlight when their kisses ended was reserved only for him.

He'd been a fool. She'd had *a few* special loves in her life. Part of him couldn't help but wonder if what she'd shared with another man was as special as what they'd shared together. Was it that egotistical of him to want that?

They started the ride back in silence, almost as they had been on the ride from the airport to Steerage Rock. Except Mandy wasn't quite hugging the door to keep from being close to him. But she wasn't sitting snug up against him like she did when they were together, and suddenly Beau realized that was exactly what he wanted.

"Have you seen your family much since you've been home?" she asked finally.

Small talk, he realized. Mandy had never met his brothers or his parents. Beau had been too fearful to tell them of his relationship lest his father take revenge on Hank Promise's niece. But he'd talked to Mandy about them a lot.

"I see Brock and Jack some. Cody is too much like my father to see past anything I do, so I steer clear of him when he gets his gander up."

The shift to talk about his family made Beau's insides burn. They weren't the typical Brady Bunch family.

"What about your parents?"

"Mom died a few years back," he said in a low voice. The words caught in his throat and made it hard to swallow as it did every time he talked of his mother. Despite his father's mean spirit, Eleanor Gentry loved the man, although Beau had a hard time seeing how. And she loved her boys and ranching.

Mandy reached across the seat and placed a gentle hand on his arm. "I'm so sorry, Beau."

Her voice was filled with emotion he knew was genuine.

He nodded, as he didn't trust his voice to say much more.

When he finally felt the emotion pass, he went on. "It was a stupid accident. I guess she was climbing a ladder to straighten a picture on the wall and slipped. Broke her neck and died instantly. Brock found her."

"How horrible."

Beau had to agree. He knew his kid brother had gone through some rough times after finding his mother dead like that. He'd been so young, barely ten when Beau left on the road, and just shy of fifteen when they'd lost his mom.

"It must be so hard for your father."

"I wouldn't know," he said harshly.

He didn't look at her. Didn't want to see the shocked look on her face. Despite knowing how much Mike Gentry despised Hank Promise, Mandy had never been able to understand how he could toss aside his family for something as frivolous as land. And because she didn't understand, she'd never understand the decisions Beau had made over the last eight years where his family was concerned.

"You're not telling me you haven't seen your father since you've been back, are you?"

"I've been busy."

"Too busy to talk to your father?"

"Let's not discuss this, Mandy."

"Why not? You came running to Hank's side, but you haven't even taken five lousy minutes to see your own dad. What does that say?"

"We said what we had to say to each other a long time ago. There's nothing more to say."

"I don't believe that."

"Believe what you want, Mandy. You just don't understand."

"Well, then try me. I'd like to understand."

He glanced at her and for a split second he saw the girl she was eight years ago. The girl who believed that love could conquer all, who believed that what was good and right about the world would prevail over bad. He saw Mandy, the woman who'd taken his heart and shut the door to any others who'd come along since.

"He didn't call me to tell me my mother had died," he said, past the tightness and anger lodged in his throat. "Cody called me three days after the funeral because I never showed. Was madder than a bull chasing a rodeo clown because he thought I didn't care enough to come home to my own mother's funeral. Dad told my brothers he'd take care of calling me, but he never did it."

"My God, how could he have done that to you?"

"How? Because that's Mike Gentry. Never forgave me for 'siding with the enemy' or for leaving the ranch to go rodeo. He never forgets, and he always pays you back for the wrongs you do to him. Denying me the right to say good-bye to my mother with the rest of the family was my payback for leaving."

"You've never spoken to him since then?"

It took a moment for the old wounds to close up and for his heart rate to calm to a steady beat again. He waited until he could trust himself to speak. "I left as soon as Cody called. Went to Mom's grave and saw all the flowers from the funeral wilting in the hot sun. I couldn't believe she was lying there underneath it all." He wondered if his heartache would ever fade. These days he didn't fall to the ground and cry like a baby as he had then. But the years hadn't made talking about the loss of his mother any easier.

Beau wasn't a man who admitted his emotions much. Like all the Gentry boys, he'd been taught by the strap and the harsh word to be a man. *Cowboys don't cry.* He'd never seen gentleness in any man until he'd met Hank Promise.

The hand Mandy held on his arm tightened. He didn't want to look at her, didn't want her to see the shame he felt in not being there for his mother. For leaving her and not coming back. Lord only knew why she'd loved Mike Gentry or how she'd put up with his ways for so many years. She'd deserved more.

"Dad found me at her grave," he went on. "It was almost like he was waiting for me there in the shadows, waiting to have the last say again." Beau shook his head, trying to will the memories and hatred away. "I told him I'd lost my beloved mother and as far as I was concerned I had no father. They were the last words I ever spoke to him."

Mandy was quiet for a long while.

"You were angry."

"It was much more than anger."

"Hurt, yes, I know. He hurt you badly. You were both hurting. It may not be the same for us, but I do know how you feel."

He glanced at her then and his heart did a flip. "Yeah, you do, don't you. But your dad would never do something so coldhearted to you."

She shook her head. "No, he wouldn't. And

things aren't as bad as they used to be with us. It wasn't always easy for me to accept some of my father's ways, but we've worked through a lot. It's easier now. Maybe because I'm older. I don't know. Maybe now that some time has passed you should try to talk to your father—"

"No!"

"You were both hurting. People do terrible things sometimes when they're in pain."

"He's still the same man. And what's worse is he's turning my brother Cody into the same stock."

"Beau."

"Forget it, Mandy, it was in the past. Any feelings I have for that man I've just shut off and left behind."

She just stared at him until he turned to look at her. He could see it in her eyes, the questions, the conclusions she was coming to. *Was it that easy to let go of us, too?*

He wanted to say the words out loud. Tell her that, no, it had nearly killed him to leave her behind. He'd had no choice. As he drove out of Texas that day, he'd prayed that they'd both find happiness some day without each other. Because he knew his father would make it impossible for them to be happy together. It had taken all his strength to keep from turning around and racing to the airport to catch her before she left his life forever.

But he'd clung to the hope that Mandy would eventually be happier without him. That's what had kept him moving forward even when he doubted his decision to leave her.

The rain had subsided some since they'd left the cabin. Although Beau had the urge to gun it back to the ranch, he took it slow to keep from getting caught in a rut and sliding off the muddy road. The windshield wipers whined as they smacked back and forth. Mandy had her window open to catch what little relief from the heat she could despite having the rain whipping her in the face.

He couldn't help himself. He had to ask.

"You never answered me, Mandy."

She crinkled her nose into an adorable frown.

"Have you been happy these last eight years? I mean really happy?"

She tossed him a wry grin. "You mean the kind of happy that follows you around like the moon?"

He chuckled. "Yeah, something like that."

"Beau, that's a fairy tale and you know it."

His heart fell deep in his chest. "Happiness isn't a fairy, tale, Mandy. It's getting up and knowing where you are and where you want to go and feeling good about it. It's not something that only people in books have. You deserve that, too."

"Are you happy?"

"Sometimes."

She looked at him thoughtfully and he wondered if she was thinking of what had been between them. What could have been. He knew he'd been thinking a whole lot about it these last few days.

Easing the truck down an embankment toward the creek, Beau groaned out loud.

Mandy took in the expression on Beau's face, already not liking what it meant. "Is it bad?"

"Ruts are filled with water. The tires are skidding."

Mandy remained quiet and let Beau concentrate on his driving. If they skidded off the road, it would be an easier walk back up to the cabin than all the way back to the ranch. It was late enough in the day that she knew Beau would take the alternative to head to the cabin over heading home. That wasn't an option for her.

Raindrops pounded on the roof of the truck, making her ears ring. The windshield wipers whipping to and fro did little to help the visibility. Mandy kept her window open and moved toward the middle of the cab. It was easier to see the bank of the road through the open window, despite the rage of rain flying into the truck.

"Don't go too close to this side of the road."

"I'm trying to keep her steady in the middle, but already the ground is like a mud pit. Oh, no," Beau said, groaning. He slowed down as they made it to the bottom of the hill and rolled down his window all the way to look outside.

"What's wrong?" Mandy asked, not being able to see anything in the direction Beau was now looking.

"Cattle are one of the most beautiful of all God's creatures and sure as spit they're the dumbest."

After stopping the truck in the center of the washed-out road, Beau pushed open the door.

"Why do you say that?"

"One of the cows broke from the herd and decided to birth her calf in the middle of the swamp. A swamp, for crying out loud! She could have had the whole mountain and she chooses here and now of all times to give birth."

"It's not like she had a choice of when, Beau," Mandy said, moving over to the driver's side so she could look in the direction Beau was pointing.

"No, but she could have chosen a more practical spot to have her miracle. Like one I wouldn't have to wade through to go rescue her baby. If I don't get that calf out of there, her momma will never be able to once the creek rises. The calf will end up drowning."

"Oh, no. Then we have to get her."

"Keep yourself dry in the truck. I'll take care of it."

"I'm already soaking wet."

The rain was so loud as it hit the roof of the truck that Mandy didn't heard the plaintive mooing of the cow or the much softer call of her calf until she slid out of the truck and slammed the door. She followed on Beau's heels down toward the creek. The water was rising steadily. Even Mandy could tell the difference between now and when they'd first driven up to the cabin. It was only a matter of time before the banks were flooded and the entire area around them would be under water.

She carefully stepped over rotten stumps and twigs toward the calf.

"You should have stayed in the truck," Beau said. "This ground is like a sponge. You're liable to lose a boot in this mud bog."

*Too late.*

"Ah, Beau?"

He halted his stride a few yards ahead of her and angled back, tossing her a questioning glance beneath the rim of his cowboy hat.

Mandy just smiled sheepishly, trying her best to stand steady on one foot.

Beau shook his head and chuckled as he strode back up the embankment toward her. "I will never understand the female species," he muttered.

"You don't have to understand them to enjoy them," she said, smiling wickedly.

Had she really said that? It felt so natural a comeback, like the easy banter they'd shared years ago. She was flirting with him, she realized, and the twinkle in his eyes told her he knew it. What surprised her more was that she actually liked the feeling of flirting with Beau again.

Beau walked past her to the point where she'd stepped out of her boot. As he pulled it from the muck, it made a sucking sound. He shook it a few times to rid it of mud, but it didn't seem to help all that much.

He was laughing as he stooped down in front of her to help her put it back on. She couldn't keep her own laughter at bay either.

"I can't guarantee it'll be clean and dry when you put your foot back in it, Cinderella, but there's nothing I can do about it just this second, short of carrying you to the truck and—"

"That won't be necessary," she insisted. Placing her hands on his shoulders to steady herself, she said, "Just help me get my foot into the boot and I'll live with the mud and grit."

He was touching her foot. When she'd stepped out of her boot her sock had half slipped off with it and now Beau gently pushed it back up into place. The feel of his hand on her seemed too intimate. She'd never thought of her foot as being at all sensual, but the care with which Beau touched her and eased her boot back into place made her suddenly feel light-headed. She wondered vaguely if this was how Cinderella felt having her glass slipper placed on her foot by the prince.

Chuckling to herself as she put her foot back down on the ground, Mandy decided that she may have one thing in common with Cinderella, but she was sure the fairy-tale princess hadn't found herself in the pouring rain having to rescue a calf in a swamp afterward.

"Go back to the truck," Beau called out as he headed back down the embankment.

"You may need my help."

"Stubborn woman," he said, laughing as he shook his head.

The cow didn't like them getting too close to her baby. That much was evident by the way she stomped her hooves and paced around them, mooing her protest. The calf, who had to have been born mere hours ago, was barely able to get his footing in the mud. Mandy wasn't doing much better. All the while the momma cow was mooing loud and eyeing Beau as he eased the calf into his arms.

As Beau started up the embankment, he hit a flow of mud and started sliding backward.

"Hold on to her, Beau."

The look on Beau's face was truly hilarious as he struggled to keep his balance, hold on to an agitated calf, and avoid coming in contact with a more than distraught mother cow as he inched up the small incline.

"Do you need me to help?"

"I got her," he called out. "She's a good kicker. You might get hurt. Just keep an eye on her momma. She's not looking too happy right now."

Mandy couldn't help but laugh. Beau's cowboy hat was tilted to one side, giving his face no protection from the pouring rain. The calf was calling out to her momma. The cow looked ready to charge on Beau, if only she could make it up the hill without sliding back down.

As they made it to the road, the calf's agitation grew and she began kicking furiously. Beau held on tight, but in an effort not to drop the calf, he ended up stepping right out of his boots and landing on his back in the mud, cradling the calf on his chest. His hat had fallen off behind him in the mud and was now face-up, collecting rain.

"She's okay now," Mandy said, trying to stifle a laugh.

Beau released the calf. Immediately it went in search of its mother, who had finally made it up to the road. The cow let out a long moo.

"You're welcome," Beau called out, glaring at the cow, who was still perturbed at him even though her calf was now out of danger and strutting slowly back to her.

Mandy held her wet hand to her lips to hide the smile she couldn't control.

"Stupid cow," Beau muttered, looking around himself for his hat.

It had been raining steadily, but now another wave of heavy rain came down on them. Beau emptied his hat of rain-water and stuffed it on his head, all the while continuing to search the area around him.

"Where are my boots?!" he barked out.

Unable to contain herself any longer, Mandy burst out laughing, doubled over in merriment.

"I'm glad you think this is so funny. Those are my favorite boots," Beau said, laughing himself. He was positively covered with mud when he stood up in his stockinged feet. He grabbed his boots, which were soaked and mud-stained, and stood staring. His devilish grin made her pause.

"What is spinning in that head of yours, Beau Gentry?" she said in what she hoped was warning enough to keep him from doing what she thought he was about to do.

"You're too clean."

"No, I'm very dirty. Remember, I lost my boot in the mud, too. I'm very wet and very dirty."

She started backing up slowly, then faster when she realized that without footwear, there was nothing to slow down Beau's stride.

"You need a little more mud, Mandy."

"You wouldn't dare."

"You know I would." And he did. Before she could spin on her heels and race back to the truck, Beau had picked up a handful of mud and, catching up to her, he smeared it on her. Then he retreated before she could reach him and counter the attack. The glob of muck oozed down the right side of her hat, tilting it so that half the mud dripped down her ear and neck.

"You dirty rat!" she said, laughing until she couldn't tell if the tears on her face were from laughter or rain.

Bending down she quickly tried to toss a ball of mud in his direction as she rounded the side of the truck, hoping to gain some cover. It landed pitifully on the hood.

It was one thing to fling mud on the outside of the truck, but she was sure Beau would take pains not to muddy her inside the cab. Dripping with mud and wet to the bone, she yanked open the passenger side door and crawled in. The second after she slammed the door shut, Beau climbed into the driver's seat and slammed the door. Both of them were laughing, so hard that her sides hurt.

"Look at my boots," Beau said, muttering as he dropped them on the floor.

It was too much for her to take. Rain was dripping down his face, dragging strands of hair into his eyes and matting it against his face. A drop of water made a slow trail from the corner of his eye, down his cheek, and rested just to the side of his chiseled chin next to a smudge of mud. Mandy had the unbelievable urge to touch him there, kiss that drop of water from his face. She wanted to bury herself in his arms, lose herself in his kisses, and feel her heart collide with his.

Instead she stared at him, at the drop of water on his face, at his slightly parted lips and the way his chest rose and fell with each breath he dragged in. Mud and all, he was incredibly handsome. She wanted to reach across the cab of the truck, which suddenly seemed way too big and much too small for anything she had in mind.

"Are you okay?" he asked. His voice was low, and smooth as a calm pond on a breezeless day. And he was staring back at her with the same intensity she felt inside herself.

"Yes."

"You sure about that?"

No, she wasn't okay. What she was feeling right now was a raging storm of emotion that would surely lead her back to heartbreak.

"What I said before about there being others."

Beau's expression grew tight. "It doesn't matter," he said, leaning across the space between them and placing his hand on her cheek, gently brushing it. His fingers felt gritty, but his touch turned her knees to jelly and sent shock waves through her whole body.

"Yes, it does," she said quietly, her mouth suddenly bone-dry. She wanted to lean into his touch, kiss his palm. Instead, she just enjoyed the new feelings his touch evoked.

He smiled, slow and sexy, and her heart did a flip.

"I guess I got a little carried away. You have mud on your face. In your hair," he whispered.

He tipped her hat off her head with his other

hand and tossed it to the floorboards. All the while he kept his hand on her cheek, brushing away the gritty wet dirt.

"I'm making it worse."

Shaking her head slightly, she said, "No, you're not."

"I shouldn't be touching you this way."

He started to pull his hand away, but Mandy held it in place against her cheek.

His eyes were dark and filled with longing. "Mandy, I want to kiss you."

"Then kiss me," she whispered back.

She let herself go. She met him halfway, draping her arms around his shoulders. There was no room for indecision. She wanted to kiss Beau, and by the way his mouth moved to meet hers, the way he dug his fingers into her matted hair until it tumbled down to her shoulders, and cradled her body against his, he wanted to kiss her, too.

She opened up to him, not sure she'd ever be able to get enough of what he had to give. Not sure if there'd ever be enough hours in a day or days in a lifetime to know all there was to know about Beau Gentry.

She wanted to be with him. Much as she'd hated it, she'd been drawn to Beau like a magnet ever since she'd set foot off that plane. It felt amazingly good to admit it to herself after all this time. It was better to feel it and be there in his arms.

The charging rain against the roof of the truck just barely drowned out her soft moan and the rampant beating of her heart. Mandy clung to Beau, to his rain-sodden clothes, feeling his hard body against hers, feeling the strength of his arms as he pulled her against his chest, setting her soul on fire.

It wouldn't last forever. She knew that. But for this moment she'd make it last, savor every bit of Beau's kisses for as long as she could.

The distance sound of a horn blaring in the distance slowly cut through the charge of the rain. Beau pulled away from her and looked into her eyes. She knew that look. It had haunted her endlessly with its memory. But before she could kiss Beau again, the noise in the distance grew louder, until it was impossible to ignore.

"What are they doing up here?" Beau released Mandy, grabbing his boots and quickly slipping into them.

It could only mean one thing, but Mandy wasn't ready to face it. Fighting her fear, she quickly threw open the door and stepped out into the rain.

Mitch's truck was stopped about a hundred

yards away. He ran through the mud-bogged road until he was halfway to Beau's truck.

"I'm so glad I caught up with you."

"What is it?" Beau asked.

Mitch could hardly catch his breath. He didn't have to utter a word for Mandy to know what he was about to say. His face said it all.

"It's Hank. He's collapsed."

## Chapter Eight

For the first time that day, Beau questioned taking Mandy away from the ranch. *Oh, Lord, if anything happened to Hank while they were gone.* He'd never forgive himself.

"We're never going to get the truck through this mud without some help," Beau said.

"I have a winch if you get stuck, but it'll take too long. Leave the truck and drive back with me."

They quickly walked the distance to Mitch's pickup and climbed inside. Mandy sat in the middle between him and Mitch, forced into tight quarters, but already Beau felt the difference between them. She was snug up against him, leaning against his body. Beau had to admit he liked this change of heart, and hoped it wasn't just out of fear for what might have happened to Hank.

She needed comfort to keep her fear at bay, and he was going to give it to her. Wrapping his arm around her shoulders, he pulled her to him so she was resting against his side. He realized immediately that he needed her comfort as much as she needed his.

As Mitch's truck bounced back down the road toward the ranch, Mandy's eyes drifted up to meet his. It nearly broke his heart. She seemed . . . shattered.

He did the only thing he could. He bent his head and pressed his lips against her forehead. "You talk to him," Beau said softly. "He'll listen to you. You're the only one he'll listen to."

Mandy nodded her head weakly.

It seemed to take forever to reach the ranch house. The sun was sinking below the trees when Mitch's truck finally pulled up out front. Knowing the doctors would take measures to operate, Hank insisted on staying home instead of going to the hospital, despite Corrine's pleas. The paramedics had stabilized him as best they could while Corrine had called his doctor. The doctor was just stepping off the porch when they climbed out of the truck.

"He's comfortable," Corrine said. It had

taken its toll on her, Beau could tell. In the time they'd been gone she looked as if she'd aged ten years.

"I want to see him," Mandy said with a sob.

"He needs to rest," Dr. Cookman said. "Don't upset him. Right now his heart is like a time bomb. Just let him rest and I'll check on him in the morning." He turned to Corrine and reaching out, squeezing her hand. "You have my direct number. You call me if you need to. I don't care what time it is."

"I will. Thank you so much, Rich."

*His heart is like a time bomb.*

Beau's ears were still ringing with Dr. Cookman's words when he left Hank's room later that evening. If Mandy couldn't convince Hank to have the surgery, he was going to lose his friend, a good man who had been like a father to him.

And Mandy would lose so much more.

The house had grown quiet now that all the hands were back at the bunkhouse.

"Let me help you with the dishes, Aunt Corrine," Mandy said. She needed something to do, something to keep her busy. But she suspected her aunt needed it more.

She came up from behind, wrapped her arms around her aunt, and felt her shoulders shudder.

After a few moments, Corrine sobbed, "When I was lying in bed with him earlier I thought, 'Lord, how many more times am I going to be able to have him here in my arms like this?' I thought we were going to lose him today for sure."

"I know. I should have been here."

"No, you can't stop your life just because he's being so stubborn. None of us can."

"I wish . . ."

"What, doll?"

She slumped down into a kitchen chair and mindlessly twirled an empty glass between her fingers. "I should have come more often."

"Oh, don't go there again. You have a life of your own. No one expects you to give it up."

Mandy chuckled wryly. "I wish my mother would say that."

Her aunt looked down at the soapsuds and stilled. "I didn't want to call your mother and tell her about Hank. In fact, he asked me not to. Was quite cross with me for doing it."

Mandy closed her eyes and shook her head. "He's such a . . ." She paused, searching for the right word. Then, looking up at her aunt, they both said in tandem, "cowboy."

"I'm glad you made that call. Otherwise, I may have never known until it was too late. For that I'm sorry. Some niece I turned out to be."

"You're wonderful for him. We both love you so very much."

"Can I ask you something personal?"

"Anything."

"How come you and Uncle Hank never had children? You'd both make wonderful parents."

Corrine didn't answer right away and immediately Mandy wondered if it were too painful a subject for her aunt. Her hands stilled in the dishwater.

"I would have loved to have had a child with Hank," she said quietly. "It wasn't in God's plan, I guess."

"You could have adopted. I can just see Hank and a string of young cowboys out in the barnyard. He was always so great with me, always encouraged me and made me feel like I could do anything. You'd make a terrific mother, too. I remember so many nights when I first came to the Double T I'd cry myself to sleep and you always stayed by my side. You and Hank are like a second set of parents to me."

Corrine was quiet and Mandy was afraid she'd hurt her aunt's feelings. But then she turned and smiled at Mandy, her eyes filled with tears.

"We didn't need to adopt a child. We were blessed with you."

Mandy swallowed the lump in her throat. She

was well loved by the people in her life. How many people could say that? And yet, she thought back to what Beau had asked her about being happy. Was she?

"And you both were happy?"

"We have each other. You could drive yourself crazy with what-would-have-beens if you let it get to you. But yes, I've always been happy. And I think up until recently, Hank's been happy, too."

Mandy pushed herself out of her chair. "I don't doubt it. If Uncle Hank doesn't care about himself, he can't be happy about what this is doing to everyone else."

Her aunt's shoulders slumped. "He has his reasons, not that I agree with him. But they are his own."

"Why don't you tell me what they are?"

Corrine turned to her, unshed tears still clinging to her eyelids. "You need to ask him that yourself, doll. Only he can tell you."

Mandy picked up a dish towel and started wiping one of the dishes her aunt had set to dry on the rack. Her aunt quickly stilled her hand.

"Please leave them. I need some busywork to do and if I don't have any to keep me occupied I'll go crazy. As it is, I'll probably be tearing at this house until the morning sun."

"Okay," Mandy said, understanding. "I'm going to check on Uncle Hank before I turn in."

She kissed her aunt's cheek and left the kitchen, listening to her heart beating and the loud drum of blood rushing through her veins. As she crossed the living room to the stairway, she paused and angled back to the fireplace mantle where the pictures of her and Uncle Hank and Aunt Corrine were carefully placed.

Walking over to the mantel, she chose the picture of her sitting on her uncle's lap when they visited his mother on the reservation. The day she'd met Alice's daughter Sara. There was something about that picture that had given her pause when she'd seen it the other day. If she looked at it quick enough. . . .

*We didn't need to adopt. We were blessed with you.*

With trembling hands, she took the picture from the mantel and stared at it again. Then she climbed the stairs to the second floor. When she reached Hank's bedroom, she knocked lightly on the door.

"Are you up for company?" she asked, when she poked her head in.

"Always for you," Hank said, lifting his arm up in invitation for her to join him on the bed. He was sitting up, his face ghostly white and his breathing better now that he'd had a little rest. The doctor said it would get better as long as he didn't overdo it.

"I need you, you big ninny," she said, tears blurring her vision. She settled into his arms, resting her head on his broad shoulders like she used to when she was a young girl. He enfolded her in his arms and gave her a squeeze. He always gave her the hugs she craved, always made her feel accepted, gave his approval willingly, endlessly. She had the feeling she could do no wrong in her uncle's eyes.

"You don't need me, darlin'. You're all grown up and taking the world by the ears and making them listen to you now. You've got your momma's brains."

Her eyes fell to the photo in her hand. *And my grandmother's eyes.* She gazed up at Hank and saw for the first time with the eyes of a woman what she would never see—could never see—as a child.

She swallowed hard before daring to speak, feeling her bottom lip tremble. But it was too important to ignore. "How come you never told me you're my real father?" she asked, her voice low and thick with emotion.

She took a deep breath and waited with trepidation for his reply.

Hank's arm tightened just a fraction around her and his body tensed. His eyes suddenly filled with a sheen of moisture and she saw what looked to her like regret. "How. . . ."

Her voice was shaky when she spoke and she fought mightily to keep it steady. "I guess it's always been there. Mom and Dad fighting endlessly, always just before I came to Texas. You and Aunt Corrine were supposed to be such good family friends, except you and my parents never spend any time together, only when it has to do with me. All the clues were there when I was growing up, except if you aren't looking for something, you won't find it. And if you don't want to see it, you'll just push any evidence of it aside."

She paused, swallowing hard after the words rushed out of her mouth. He hadn't denied it. It could only mean one thing. She fought to keep from bursting into tears and making what was already difficult for both of them even harder.

"I'm all grown up, Uncle Hank. I can read things differently and I can handle what I may not have been able to accept when I was seven." She smiled, handing him the picture she'd brought to the room. "I have my grandmother's eyes."

His eyebrows knitted.

"Remember that first day we met at my recital?"

"How could I ever forget?"

"You told me your name was Hank Promise and I told you my name was Promise, too. Mandy Promise Morgan. You smiled and said I had my grandmother's eyes. The only other person who ever said that to me was Mom. When I was a kid, I didn't think anything of it. Why would I? But Mom's mother had big hazel-green eyes, just like hers. And Dad's eyes are blue and . . . he was adopted. Did you know that?"

Hank shook his head.

"No one would have known what color eyes his biological mother had. My eyes aren't quite like yours, but they're an awful lot like this picture of your mother. I think I look a little like her."

Hank closed his eyes and breathed in deeply, his bottom lip trembling. Mandy instantly regretted bringing up the subject, fearing it would be too hard for Hank to handle.

"I gave your mother my word. It was the only way."

Tears fell unchecked down her face, blurring her vision.

"The only way my father would allow you to be part of my life? Being adopted himself, I think it was important for Dad to have me all to himself. When you came into my life, he had to share me. With you."

"It had been years since I'd seen your mother. I was just outside Philadelphia for a rodeo. I was sitting there at some diner reading the morning paper over breakfast with some other cowboys when I saw you staring up at me from the newspaper. You were standing beside your mother and your piano instructor, getting ready for a recital. I saw those big brown eyes and knew without a doubt you were my daughter."

Mandy laughed through the tears. "I remember that day. I'd never seen a cowboy before. I remember thinking you were so big with that black cowboy hat and boots you always wore. I was so afraid to talk to you. You told me not to be afraid, you were my uncle from Texas."

The corners of Hank's mouth lifted into a wide grin. "You didn't even question it. You just asked me where Texas was, like it was a million miles away. When I drove out of Philadelphia that day it sure felt like a million miles."

"You gave me a yellow rose to bring onstage when it was my turn to play and told me to smile pretty, that you'd be standing in the back of the room listening. And you did, because I watched. After I was done playing mom asked me where I'd gotten the pretty rose, and I told her you gave it to me and that your name was Promise just like mine. I thought she'd faint right there."

Hank shrugged. "It wasn't exactly the smoothest way for me to introduce myself into your life."

Mandy also recalled how for days afterward she would go to bed and hear her parents argue endlessly. She'd felt guilty and asked her mother if she'd done something wrong for talking to Hank because he was a stranger and was that the reason they were arguing. She said no, that Mandy hadn't done anything wrong. But she explained how Uncle Hank was not really a relative, but instead a good friend of the family that she hadn't seen in a long time. Her mother also said she'd probably be seeing more of him and that Mandy should still call him Uncle Hank.

After that Hank would come to visit for birthday parties or special occasions and her parents fought for days afterward. They never kissed and made up the way she always thought grownups kissed and made up when they had fights.

Then, at the end of the fourth grade, just before she went to Texas for the first time, her father didn't talk to anyone for a week. When she boarded the plane with her mother, he just looked at her and told her everything would be okay when she came home. And it was. It always was.

"I never wanted to cause any pain to you or your folks, Mandy. I just. . . ."

"I'm glad I know the truth," she said, thinking back over all the fights and all the bad feelings until they rolled into one big blur. "And you don't have to feel guilty about me finding out. Mom must have wanted me to know someday. Otherwise, why would she have given me your name?"

A fresh set of tears stung the inside of her eyelids, spilling down her cheek. Hank kissed her forehead and squeezed her tight, holding her in silence for a long moment.

"I meant what I said, Uncle Hank. I need my father in my life."

"You have a father," he interjected quickly. "I can't take any credit for raising you or making you into the woman you've become. Sometimes I think it would have made things a lot easier for all of you if I'd stayed away."

"I'm glad you didn't. I can't imagine not having you in my life."

"You're not angry then?"

"No, not angry. To be honest, I don't know exactly what I feel. I'm a little numb. But it explains a lot. Like why I could never do anything completely right in my father's eye. To him I could have always done better. Maybe I could never live up to what he wanted because I wasn't . . . really his daughter."

"Stop that. He loves you and raised you like his own. Having his blood wouldn't have changed things. It's just the kind of man he is. He's always going to be your daddy."

"I know that. But you still have a special place in my life. That's why I don't understand why you won't have the surgery. Whatever relationship we have is ours and ours alone, no matter how it's defined. You're an important part of my life and I don't want to lose you. Do you regret what happened with you and mom?"

"Never. It brought you into my life. But I sometimes regret how things ended for us. Your mom used to be . . . happier. She was a different woman when I knew her. Sometimes I wonder about things, but that can drive a person crazy. How do you go back? Which part of who you are now would you give up to go back and fix things? I love Corrine different from the way I loved your mother, but still as special."

Hank drew in a deep breath and was quiet a moment, just staring at her face. Mandy wondered what he was thinking as he looked at her for the first time, knowing she knew the truth.

"So much of this has been playing through my head these last few days," he said. "I couldn't face going under the knife without you knowing. Except I gave your mother my word. . . ."

Mandy sat up in bed, swiped the tears from her cheeks, and looked squarely at him. "Well, now I know. And you didn't break any promises to Mom. I'm going to be right here with you and Aunt Corrine while you have your surgery. Please . . . please say you'll have it. I can't bear the thought of losing you."

He gazed at her for a short while, his eyes waging war with fear and regret and renewed hope. "Okay, doll. I'll do it."

Hank was asleep when she left his room. Corrine was waiting by the door. In her hands was a dishrag she was winding tighter than a toothpick.

"Call Dr. Cookman and tell him Hank will be in the hospital early tomorrow for the surgery," Mandy said.

The relief on her aunt's face was instantaneous. She held Mandy's gaze for a long moment, but didn't ask the question that was written in her eyes.

Mandy nodded. "He told me the truth."

Wrapping their arms around each other, they sobbed.

## Chapter Nine

A short time later, Corrine was settled in with Hank. An ambulance was due to pick Hank up at sunrise to take him to the hospital. Her uncle may have been the one who was ill, but her aunt was emotionally exhausted.

Mandy was spent, too, but she couldn't go to sleep now if she tried. Hank was going to have surgery. He was going to be all right. It was a tremendous relief. But she couldn't feel any of it just yet.

*Which part of who you are now would you give up to go back and fix things?* Mandy couldn't get Hank's words out of her head.

These feelings she had for Beau were just as strong as they were eight years ago. At times she thought they were more so. But maybe they couldn't go back either. They'd both changed and grown into two different people. Her life was now in Philadelphia. In a few short weeks when Hank was on his feet again, Beau would go back to the rodeo to compete for the World Championship. *It had been his dream.*

She walked down the dirt path to the bunk-house, chiding herself for needing to see Beau. The sounds of male bonding on the inside of the bunkhouse drifted out into the night air. This wasn't her place, but she knocked anyway.

"What's wrong, Mandy?" Beau asked, greeting her at the door with arms opened wide. Just for her. Thank God he was here with her. She'd held it together as long as she could, but now her head was swimming.

Her father wasn't really her father. Hank was the man responsible for bringing her into the world. It explained so much. And yet . . . oh, God, life as she knew it wasn't anything she thought it was at all.

She slipped into his arms naturally and held on. He smelled fresh and clean from the shower he'd taken earlier when they'd come back from the cabin.

Mandy glanced past Beau's shoulder and saw the hands seated at the card table. Bottles of beer were lined up in a row. A pile of dollar bills and loose change were thrown in the center of the table. Each hand had their own stash by their side.

"Can you get away for a walk?" she asked, looking up at Beau's face. She knew the ritual of cowboy poker. Today had been a particularly hard day physically and emotionally for the hands and the family. It was a way for them to regroup. Beau was part of this ritual even if she wasn't.

"Just let me get a coat for you. You look cold," Beau said.

She wasn't cold, but she realized then that she was shivering. She'd left Hank's room without a thought to where she was going and ended up at the bunkhouse. She'd been hoping Beau hadn't turned in yet. She needed to have him hold her, needed to be comforted by his embrace and his strength.

She turned away from the doorway and heard Beau tell the hands to deal him out of this game. After a few rumbles and groans, Beau was by her side, draping a denim jacket over her shoulders. She leaned her cheek into the soft cotton and inhaled the smoky scent, still lingering on the fibers after burning mesquite the other day.

They walked in silence, seemingly following the moonlight. Each intake of breath propelled them forward until they ended up by a grassy clearing beyond the calving barn. The sounds of crickets and horses filled the air around them.

"Everything all right with Hank?" Beau finally asked, dropping to the ground. She followed him and he immediately enfolded her in his arms. Memories of Beau holding her earlier in the day filled her head. They'd been so good together, so right. How could she suddenly feel so disjointed?

"He's sleeping. Aunt Corrine is with him, too. I hope she gets some sleep herself; she looks like she's about to collapse. He's finally agreed to have the surgery," she said quietly, her bottom lip trembling. She wasn't sure if it was from relief or from fear. Or maybe because of the news she'd just learned.

The heavy sigh of relief lifted his chest, squeezing her in his tight embrace. But Mandy didn't mind at all. If she never left Beau Gentry's arms, she'd die a happy woman. She forced away the nagging reminder that crawled to the surface of her mind that they would soon be going their separate ways.

"There's more." This time the trembling of her lips accompanied a fresh set of tears brimming in her eyes.

Beau tipped up her chin. "What is it? What's wrong?"

Mandy couldn't seem to get the words past

her throat. It had been easier to confront Hank. She wasn't sure why. Maybe because there'd been so much at stake. But now. . . .

"Hank is my father, Beau."

Silence.

"Did you hear what I said? All this time I've been trying to please my father, not getting his approval for anything, when I always had the approval of my father. Hank is my real father."

"I know."

Shocked, she blinked away the tears and glanced up at him. "You-you know?"

He nodded.

"But how did you. . . . How long have you known?"

He held her gaze even as he hesitated. "Eight years."

Pulling from his embrace, Mandy abruptly stood up, brushing the wet blades of grass from her jeans. "You knew the truth all this time and you never told me?" she asked accusingly.

Beau remained in place on the grass, leaning back on his arms as he looked up at her. "It wasn't for me to tell. That was Hank's secret."

"Did . . . did Hank tell you this?"

"No, my father did."

"Your father? How would he know?"

"Who knows. He probably hired a private investigator and was hoping to use that information to get back at Hank. He'd called it his ace in the hole against that thieving Apache. That's what he's always called Hank."

"I guess that makes me the thieving Apache's daughter. I was your ace in the hole?" she said bitterly.

"No, never!"

In the moonlight, she could see he was angry. He got to his feet and stood directly in front of her.

"I told you I never did anything to hurt Hank. My father wanted me to dig up dirt on him. Said if he couldn't find something that would ruin the ranch, he'd find something more personal to ruin Hank with. I didn't believe my father's accusations so I told Hank what my father was planning to do."

"And he didn't deny it," Mandy said quietly, nibbling on her bottom lip to steady it.

"No. I wasn't about to let my father's viciousness hurt you, Mandy. Don't you see, I wasn't working in cahoots with my father. I came out to the ranch to learn as much as I could about bronc riding. Because I loved being here. Hank has given me a lot. I owe him. But anything I took from him he gave willingly. I'm grateful for him for all he's done."

"If you could go to Hank with this, why couldn't you tell me?"

"You're talking about something different here."

"Am I? You made me think we were a lie. You told me you didn't love me and you were only using me."

"You know how much I regret that."

"That's not the point. Regardless of your loyalty to my uncle . . . my father, oh, God, you didn't have to lie to *me,* Beau. Not about us."

"Yes, I did."

"Why? I just don't understand it."

"My father was so bent on destroying Hank in any way he could. It had been his obsession ever since Hank bought this spread. Mike Gentry didn't care if he alienated his own sons in the process, much less the daughter of the man he hated most in the world."

"Still—"

"You needed to learn the truth from Hank, not me. And certainly not in any way my father would have represented it. And I guarantee it wouldn't have been pretty."

"I found out anyway, Beau. Eight years of time lost . . ."

Tears stung her eyes and she fought hard not to break down. Beau had told her at the airport there were only two things Hank had ever asked of him. Was this the first?

"Beau, did Hank ask you to leave me?"

Beau's silence was her answer.

Mandy buried her face in her hands, unable to keep her raging emotion at bay.

Beau gripped her by the shoulders, forcing her to look up at him.

"Hank asked you to leave me?"

"He didn't do it to hurt you, Mandy. He only wanted to spare your feelings."

"He knew how crushed I was when you left and—"

"Even if he hadn't it still wouldn't have changed anything. I still would have gone on the road without you, Mandy."

She sobered with his words, tears streaming down her cheeks. He hadn't really loved her. That's what he was saying, right? And if that were true, what was all this that was building between them now? She wrenched herself from his grip and took a wide step backwards.

"What was I supposed to do, Mandy?"

"You knew how I felt about you."

He nodded, a pained expression clouding his strong features. He looked broken. "You were so young. You know it was only a matter of time before we'd have taken things too far. I couldn't look at you without my heart pounding out of my chest so bad I couldn't breathe."

"So you made a choice and I wasn't it."

"You were sixteen, Mandy. Only *sixteen!*

You kept saying you were going to run away with me. You had everything ahead of you, and I had nothing to give you. Nothing but a gypsy life on the road. You could never live like that."

She chuckled dryly. "Beau, you never asked me if that was what I wanted."

"I didn't have to. No matter what you were saying, sleeping in a truck and living on the road wondering if I'd have made enough money from the next rodeo to keep us going wasn't the kind of life you would have been happy with."

He jammed his fingers through his thick hair and looked away, muttering an oath under his breath.

"You never asked me, Beau," she said quietly.

"I had nothing to offer you."

"You were all I wanted."

"Maybe right then. But in time you would have wanted more." He heaved a sigh. "I met Hank when he just got off the road from rodeo. I was about ten years old then and he'd just bought the Double T. I hated him for it because suddenly all that attention Dad had for me was focused on what he called some thieving Apache who stole his land.

"After one day in particular, when Dad begged off a fishing trip with me and Cody for the umpteenth time so he could meet with yet another lawyer, I decided to take my horse out to the Double T to see what was so special about it that it took Dad's every waking thought."

Mandy folded her arms across her chest and waited for him to continue.

"It was this gorgeous day after a string of lousy weather. Just perfect for being outside in the sunshine. I rode out to the top of the hill on the edge of our spread and looked around. It was real pretty land, but nothing better than what we had, and I couldn't figure out why my dad wanted it so badly. Or why he'd let it get in the way of us. I rode onto the Double T and thought I was being quiet and sneaky, thought no one saw me trespassing, until Hank came up alongside me out of nowhere."

Beau laughed in remembrance. "I was terrified, thought I'd really be in deep muck for trespassing. But Hank just said it was a beautiful day for riding, asked me if I wanted to join him while he checked out the pasture where the cattle were grazing. I felt stupid, and feeling a little low as I was, I said yes.

"Anyway, while we were riding, Hank didn't say a word. I was sure he was going to ream me at some point and was just torturing me with his silence."

Mandy couldn't help but chuckle at that.

Hank had a good way of letting you know what he was feeling just in a single look. He was also a true cowboy. Words were only spoken when necessary.

"But he never did," Beau continued. "And then I did something really stupid. I asked him why he stole my father's property. It was a stupid question because it was never my dad's to begin with, but Hank didn't make me feel stupid. He just said that my dad could have had it if he'd have wanted it bad enough. Hank had wanted it bad enough and that's why he got it."

She tried to think back on that time. When Beau was ten and she was only six. That was right about the time Hank had come into her life.

"I asked him what made him want it that bad. He told me about traveling around with the rodeo and not having a home, living in run-down motels and eating when you could in the front of a dusty old pickup. It's no life for someone who needs a home. But someday, you want to stop roaming and find that home. Someday, no matter how much you love the road, something makes you stop and want to settle down.

"So one day after school I came by when I should have been home doing chores. Hank had just finished riding a wild young bronc. I was so amazed. He said that if I wanted to ride, I had to want it bad." Beau shrugged. "I didn't know anything about getting on a horse that wasn't broke. But Hank said to come on over and he'd teach me everything I needed to know."

She smiled at that, trying to imagine a ten-year-old Beau riding for the very first time.

"Wait, you said you were ten? I thought you started training with Hank the year we met."

"I did. I went back to the Double T after school the next day and Hank gave me the afternoon. I must have seemed pretty pathetic, but he never said a word. I was so excited when I got home and told my parents about it. My mother got real quiet, but my dad . . . well, I ended up with a broken arm."

"Oh, my God, Beau. Because you were with Hank? Your father should be brought up on charges for what he did to you."

He shook his head and chuckled bitterly. "I told Hank the next day that I couldn't come back. Didn't tell him why, but I'm sure he figured it out. He took one look at my arm and told me no matter what I'd always have a place here at the Double T. I never forgot that. I tried working at my dad's ranch. I thought I could be happy. But after a while all I could think about was Hank Promise and rodeoing. I wanted it bad. So I came back to the Double T the year I met you. Even I knew I was too old to start training for rodeo, but I had to try."

"You were a natural," she said, thinking about all those times she'd seen him practicing with Hank, remembering the first few rodeos they'd gone to together.

Beau shrugged. "Even though I haven't been around the Double T much it's been like a second home to me, a sort of haven to hang my hat every now and then. I have Hank to thank for that."

"I can see how you'd feel loyalty to Hank, but Beau, you lied to me. You said you didn't want me in your life."

"Yeah, I did. You may not think so, but at the time it was the right thing to do. There were days I regretted leaving for missing you, and days when I knew it was absolutely the right thing to do. You'd have hated it. And while I can't change how I hurt you then, I can tell you that I've been thinking how things could be different for us now."

"I—I don't know, Beau. I just can't think of anything other than what's ahead for Hank. My head is swimming with all this."

He dragged her into his arms and held her. "I know. You've had a lot to absorb over the last couple of days. I don't want to put any more on you. I just want you to know that I'm here for you."

And he was, every step of the way. During the long hours of waiting at the hospital, when every noise, every tick of the clock seemed so much louder than it really was, Beau was there for her. She never thought just the mere touch of his hand to her shoulder or the brush of his wide hand across her back could say so much. But it did. So much more than words could ever say.

Mandy realized with absolute certainty that the hardest thing ahead of her was not Hank's recovery, but living without Beau. Again.

## Chapter Ten

Once Hank was out of surgery and Dr. Cook-man assured them he'd made it through the worst, Mandy felt safe enough to leave the hospital and go back to the Double T. Hank was sleeping peacefully, but her aunt couldn't bear the thought of leaving in case he woke in the middle of the night. She stayed by his side, assuring Mandy that she'd call as soon as Hank was awake.

Beau drove her back to the ranch in silence. Every once in a while, he'd whistle and then stop. She was sure he was thinking it would drive her crazy to hear it now, but it didn't. He'd gotten under her skin again. She'd gotten used to him whistling out of tune, tapping his foot like a hillbilly. *Being there for her.* She had gotten used to the sound of his voice and the feel of his comforting hand.

Mandy fought back tears that she'd held in for most of the day. Tears of fear for Hank's well-being. Tears for herself because she was going to miss her cowboy when she had to leave. Now that Hank had had his surgery and was going to be okay, there was no reason for her to remain at the ranch, no reason for Beau to stay either.

As the truck pulled up to the front of the farmhouse, Mandy wondered how she was going to be able to leave here and go back to Philadelphia, to the life she'd had before she'd come to Texas. Beau had asked her if she was happy in Philadelphia. With her work? Maybe. But she knew she'd been the happiest she'd been in a long time during her stay this past week at the ranch.

She could stay in Texas. That was always an option. She was grown-up now, and her parents weren't forcing her to come and go as they had when she was a child. It would shatter her father to learn she knew the truth about Hank, but now that she knew she couldn't ignore it. And someday her father would have to understand that she was a grown woman with a heart and mind of her own.

Philadelphia wasn't the only place she could get a job. She could certainly use her skills in advertising to get work in Amarillo or Fort Worth. Both would be a hike to commute, but it was doable. Anything was doable if you wanted it bad enough.

*Bad enough.* Beau had wanted rodeoing bad enough to leave her once before.

The heaviness in her chest multiplied tenfold. Even if she stayed in Texas, it wasn't going to change things. She'd be with Uncle Hank and Aunt Corrine, but as soon as they were assured Hank was on his feet and strong, Beau would be leaving Steerage Rock again. Once again without her.

The sound of a passenger side door opening pulled her from her thoughts.

Beau stood outside the truck holding his hand out to her. She slipped her hand into his, feeling the rough calluses abrasive against her softer skin. It grounded her.

"You look exhausted," he said.

"I am."

"The house is empty. Will you be okay by yourself in there, or do you want company for a while?"

She knew what he was asking. He didn't want to go down to the bunkhouse. He wanted to stay with her. After the day they'd had, she wanted so much to have Beau hold her again until all the indecision and unrest she felt was washed away. But no matter how much she wished it away, it wasn't going to change the truth. Beau was going back to the rodeo circuit in a few days and she would be going back to Philadelphia, to her job. Alone.

Mandy held his hand tight as she tugged him toward the house. "Come in for a little while?" she finally answered.

They crept through the living room in the dark and settled on the sofa together. Beau enfolded her in his arms. It was like coming home, Mandy thought. Suddenly all the missing pieces of the puzzle were magically there and fit perfectly into place. She knew without a doubt she could stay here like this forever.

Beau stroked her hair gently with his fingers and she burrowed herself deeper into his warmth.

They must have fallen asleep holding each other when an hour later the phone rang, rousing them.

As she became aware of the telephone ringing, Mandy rubbed her eyes and frantically ran to the phone expecting it to be Aunt Corrine. Expecting the worse. Her pulse hammered in her ear as she picked up the phone.

It wasn't her aunt.

It was her father.

Beau arched his back to get the kinks out, his eyes peering in the direction of Mandy's voice. He'd vaguely heard the blare of the telephone. There was no telephone in the living room, so she had to run to the kitchen to answer it.

Lord, he hoped it wasn't the hospital. During the hellacious day of waiting for Hank to make it through surgery, the doctor assured them all that Hank would have a peaceful night if there weren't any complications from the surgery.

When he reached the kitchen door, he saw Mandy leaning her hip against the counter with her back to him.

"It's been so crazy, Dad, with Hank's surgery and all. I haven't even had a chance to unpack my sketch pad much less work on any of the ideas I've had," she said.

He waited at the doorway, not wanting to listen in on the conversation, but needing to hear. As much as he dreaded the inevitable, he needed to hear her say the words.

"I'm sorry you couldn't reach me. I . . . no, I can charge the cell phone tonight so you can reach me directly. If I work on some sketches tonight, I can have them out to you by tomorrow afternoon at the earliest."

There was a moment of silence while she listened to the person on the other end of the phone. Beau could only hear his heart beating in his chest and the creak of the floorboard under his bare feet.

"If all goes well, I should be back in the office next Monday. Tuesday the latest. But that's the best I can do. I want. . . ."

*Back to the office.* The words echoed in Beau's head. Mandy was going back to Philadelphia. It shouldn't have thrown him as much as it did. He'd known all along she would be going back to her old life and he'd be going back to the circuit.

Funny how the thought of packing his things and throwing them into his pickup to head out on the road didn't appeal to him quite the same way it had when he'd first come back to Steerage Rock. He'd forgotten what it was like to sleep in the same bed every night, wake up looking at the sun coming through the window and bouncing off the same walls, and eating breakfast at the same table.

There was a time he'd thought that was boring, that he couldn't live his life tied to the Silverado Cattle Company. And maybe that was still true. He hadn't mended fences with his father since he'd come home, although he'd had ample opportunity to just drive over and say his peace.

Beau hadn't been bored at the Double T. Here he'd found a kind of peace and contentment that had been missing from his life. Sure, he missed rodeo in a bad way, but he'd been missing something else just as important for the last eight years. Something he'd found again being back in Texas at the Double T. *Being back with Mandy.*

But she wasn't staying. And pretty soon, no matter if he decided to forget about the World Championship and stay on to help Hank, she'd still be gone.

Beau leaned his shoulder against the doorjamb, watching Mandy fiddle with a long lock of her blond hair, watching how the light from the small French lamp by the telephone changed her hair all sorts of golden colors. And wondering how on earth he was going to be able to live without seeing her smiling face every day.

He reached his hand up and rubbed the spot in the center of his chest where his heart squeezed. He ached for what he was about to lose. But there was nothing he could do to stop it.

Mandy hung up the phone and he immediately stiffened. He had the vague feeling he wasn't going to like hearing what came next.

When she turned around, her face said it all. Her smile was so bright and radiant it stole his breath away. *He couldn't breathe.*

"We got the account!" she said, running to him and throwing her arms around his neck. "Hill Crest Industries loved my presentation."

"Congratulations. That's wonderful," he said, trying to keep his voice steady, not wanting to steal away any of her excitement.

"They want me to redo some of the aspects of the campaign, but here's the best part, they want me to lead the account. Can you believe it? You should have heard my father on the phone just now."

"He must be really proud of you," he said, forcing himself to smile.

"Yeah, he is."

She kissed him square on the lips and he kissed her back. Her lips were soft and moist. He drank in all that he could, feeling her soft body pressed against his, breathing in all her life and excitement. All the while, trying to feel it himself.

But try as he might, he couldn't.

Mandy finally pulled away and sighed. "I have a lot of work to do tonight. Dad wants some new sketches and I haven't done anything at all in days."

Beau's spirit plummeted. "You're going to work now?"

"I have to. I need to get something to him by tomorrow afternoon."

She hadn't had to tell him that part. He knew from hearing her end of the conversation and figured she'd probably be working tonight to get it all done. He squashed down that selfish feeling of wanting to hold her all night like they had before the phone rang, knowing that he wouldn't be now that she would be working.

Mandy went up on her tiptoes and kissed his cheek. "I don't want to disturb your sleep, so I'll go upstairs to work. I know you must be tired after today."

"So are you."

She shook her head. "Not anymore. I couldn't sleep now if I tried."

Beau pushed her rumpled hair away from her face with both hands. "I'm going to go back to the bunkhouse. If I'm here with you, I'm liable to do everything in my power to drag your attention away from what you're doing."

She smiled sheepishly.

"I don't want you to leave—" She caught herself, as if saying the words out loud made her see that leaving the Double T was imminent for both of them.

Beau gathered up all the strength he could,

trying to keep the desperation he felt from creeping into his voice. It wasn't fair to Mandy.

"I want to hold you in my arms and kiss you again, Mandy. And I don't want to stop. So if you're strong enough to keep your mind on your sketches while I'm doing that, then sure—"

"I see your point." She bent her head and gave him a coy grin.

He kissed her forehead. "Sleep in tomorrow morning. I can see to breakfast for the hands. I don't think Corrine will mind if me and Mitch have at it in the kitchen while you get some rest."

Giggling, she said, "Alice might mind, though."

Beau left her then, not bothering to look back. He'd only end up making a fool of himself by dragging her into his arms and kissing her again.

When he stepped off the porch, he saw the light in her room was already on. It would probably remain on all night. Glancing across the yard at the bunkhouse, he saw the lights were still glowing there as well. Another poker game no doubt.

Beau didn't want to play poker. He didn't want to be with anyone right now. Unsettled, he tried to think back on the times when he was younger, when he felt so dejected when his dad pushed him away. He and his brothers always took off to the cabin in the hills. Except this time, Beau knew that wouldn't rid him of this feeling of longing he had, this sudden feeling of loneliness invading his senses. It would only remind him about Mandy and how much he wanted her in his life.

Instead of turning in as he should have, he climbed into his pickup, needing something to do other than walk over to the bunkhouse and crawl into a cold bed alone. He needed to get away by himself for a while. Every broken man needed a night of torture once in a while, and this would be his. He'd head out to the hills where memories were abundant and painful at a time like this. And he'd drown himself good and deep in them.

Something caught the corner of his eye as he went to shift the truck into gear. A slice of moonlight shone into the cab and reflected off something on the floor. He reached down and gripped the small pearl comb he'd pulled from Mandy's hair the other day when he'd kissed her again for the first time.

Memories of their time alone in the hills invaded his mind. Staring long and hard at the comb, he gripped it in his hand until its teeth bit into his palm. The door to the house was still open. He could easily slip in and place it on the table for Mandy to see in the morning. He opened the glove compartment, and brushing his thumb along the ridges of the comb one more time, he tucked it inside.

Mandy was leaving Steerage Rock in a few days. All he had was a pearl comb to hold on to.

Beau gunned the engine and headed for the hills.

Mandy heard the sound of truck tires spitting gravel outside. Lifting her bedroom curtains back, she watched the red taillights of Beau's truck pass the bunkhouse and head up the narrow road leading to the hills. She let the curtain fall back into place.

She hadn't wanted Beau to leave. The phone call from her father was worse than awful in the timing department. But then, she and Beau never had timing on their side. He'd said he'd had no other choice since he wasn't able to reach her by cell phone. Still, she had to wonder why her father had chosen tonight of all nights to call the ranch instead of waiting until the morning.

Most probably because he knew Hank wouldn't be here, she decided as she pushed herself away from the window. She had to get to work. Despite the adrenaline rush from hearing the news from her father, she was exhausted. She wished Beau was still here. *Oh, what she wouldn't do to curl up in his arms again.*

As she pulled her sketch pad out of her bag, she realized it was probably for the best. Monday or Tuesday, she'd told her father. It was going to come quick. Probably faster than she wanted it to, despite her wanting to plant herself into her old life in Philadelphia again.

Mandy was still toiling over a sketch when she heard Beau's truck pull in sometime the next morning. He climbed out of the truck, looking worse for the wear.

She couldn't help but sigh.

Monday would come much too soon.

## Chapter Eleven

Hank's healing was good and quick to all their relief. Color returned to his face almost immediately, and the ghost that threatened to take him away from all those that loved him had disappeared. Within a matter of days he was coming home.

Mandy had called her father and told him she didn't feel comfortable leaving until she knew Hank was fully out of the woods. She didn't tell him or her mother about the conversation she'd had with Hank about him being her biological father. Some secrets needed to be kept, and this one was hers to keep with Hank.

She'd decided it would only hurt her father more to know she'd learned the truth. Make him think he'd lost her love as a daughter, when in fact, nothing had really changed. She was always going to think of Damien Morgan as her dad. She loved him, despite all the hard times they'd had. Maybe even because of them.

In true style, her father hemmed and hawed about her delayed return, but in the end took her suggestion to continue to overnight any sketches she worked on. The work kept her from having to spend too much time with Beau and face the inevitable conversation about their growing feelings for each other. And their eventual parting.

She didn't want to go there. Didn't want to have to relive the same pain she'd felt the last time she'd left Texas. She was glad to know she had her work to throw herself into to keep the memories at bay.

The night before she was due to leave she'd just finished booking her flight home when she found Beau. By the look on his face when she came out on the porch, Mandy knew Beau had already figured out what she had come to tell him.

The moon was bright, filling every space of the porch. Mandy could see every fine line on his face to the slight crease in his cotton shirt.

"I just got off the phone with my travel agent," she said.

"You going somewhere?"

His attempt at sarcasm sliced through her. "Beau, you knew this day was coming."

He was silent for a minute. "Yeah," he said quietly.

"It's good to have Uncle Hank home again. From what his doctor says, as long as he doesn't overdo things, he'll make a full recovery. We've done what we've come back to do, so there's no reason to stay."

A cloud of disappointment masked his face and she fought to see past it. Wished even more she didn't have to feel it herself.

"I guess not."

"You must be ready to get back on the road again, huh?"

"Yeah," he said tightly.

Her shoulders sagged from the weight of it all. "Don't be like this, Beau."

He looked at her directly. "You want me to make it easy for you? I'm not good at good-byes."

"That's not the way I remember it."

"It wasn't easy for me to leave you, Mandy."

"It's not easy now. For either of us," she said, looking away from his face, at the floorboards, the glider, the porch rail. Anything but his handsome face in the moonlight.

"Look, I know this is what we planned to do

when we came back to the Double T. No one wanted more than me to get Hank to have his surgery and be back out the door again. But hasn't anything between us changed things for you?"

"Of course it has. So much of this has. I can't ever think of the Double T the same as I did before I came here two weeks ago."

"And you're still leaving."

"How can it be any different between us, Beau? You said yourself I'm not the kind of woman to go roaming the country. And I realized you're right. I'm a lot like my mother that way."

She reached up and touched the light stubble on his chin, feeling the tension in his jaw from pent-up emotion. She was feeling it, too. Oh, how she wished. . . .

"My life is back in Philadelphia. After you left for the rodeo circuit, after all those dreams we'd talked about. . . . Well, I had to go on with my life. I had to forget about all that and figure out how to build my life without you. And I did that, Beau. You were right. I was just a kid falling in love for the first time. I would have followed you to the ends of the earth like a stray puppy, but eventually it wouldn't have worked. If you let yourself be honest, you'll see that it wouldn't work that way now. I'm not a rambling cowgirl. I never was. It wouldn't make me happy."

"Are you happy in Philadelphia?"

"I was happy here with you," she answered honestly. She realized she needed to say it, and Beau needed to hear it from her. "Despite everything, being with you again made me very happy."

"But."

"But we can't live our whole lives for some brief moments in Texas."

"Why can't we? Why can't you go back to Philadelphia and—"

"And catch up with you when the rodeo's in town? Or maybe when the rodeo you're in one week coincides with me having to visit a client?"

"It wouldn't have to be like that."

"I can't see how else it could be."

"So this is it for us."

She nodded, trying her best to keep herself from crying, to keep herself from taking everything that she'd said back and tell Beau that she'd follow him to the ends of the universe if it meant they'd be together. That nothing else mattered as long as they were in each other's arms.

"When's your flight leaving?" he finally asked.

She cleared her throat. "Tomorrow morning. Very early in fact. Aunt Corrine said that if anything happens, if she needs anything, she'll call right away. No matter how stubborn Uncle Hank is about it. He gave me his word, too."

"His word is good. If anything does happen, you'll call me?"

"Sure," she said, knowing there probably wouldn't be a need. Knowing too, it would take some work tracking him down, although there probably wouldn't be the need.

"I'll take you to the airport."

"It's too early. I figured I'd take the bus. That way no one will lose half a day driving me out there and back."

"I don't mind." He sighed. "I can't bring myself to say good-bye to you here."

"Okay, I appreciate it." It wasn't going to be any easier to say good-bye at the airport or anyplace else.

They stood on the front porch, under a slice of bright yellow Texas moon. They'd spent many a night in this very spot holding each other, neither wanting to let go. But as much as she wanted Beau to drag her into his arms and kiss her like there was no tomorrow, she knew it wouldn't happen. She was the one leaving this time. She absolutely refused to watch him go. And she knew he was hurting just as badly as she had all those years ago. As bad as she felt now.

"Will you make me a promise, Beau?"

"Sure. Anything."

"Go see your father before you leave?"

"Anything but that," he said tightly.

"No, Beau. That's the only thing. It's important."

"Nothing has changed."

"You don't know that. It's been a long time, Beau, and your father is getting older, too. I almost lost Hank. You don't know how much time you have left to make this right. No one knows how much time they have to say what's in their hearts. Promise me you'll try."

"I . . . I can't."

"It's all I want, Beau. All I'm asking of you."

"I can't do it, Mandy. Not even for you. It wouldn't work out."

"You don't know that if you don't try. People go their whole lives not saying what's truly in their hearts. They hurt and allow the silence to make the hurt go deeper until all you can do is put a blanket over your heart to keep from getting bitter. And even then sometimes that doesn't work."

"Is that what you did when I left?"

"Yes," she admitted. "Except seeing you

again has helped me take that blanket off again. I don't regret what we shared then or now."

Beau lifted his eyes to look at Mandy in the moonlight. Lord, she was beautiful.

"You need to tell him you love him, despite all the hurt. You need to tell him that no matter what horrible things you said to each other, he's still your dad and you love him. Because no matter what you say, I know you love your father. Otherwise, what he did wouldn't have hurt you so badly. You have to do it before his days run out and you never get the chance."

He fell silent.

"Just tell me you'll think about it before you leave. Please, for me?"

"I'll think about it."

"Thank you."

She turned much too quickly, not giving him enough time to regroup his feelings. He couldn't recall the last time he'd felt so raw and exposed.

"Mandy?"

But she was already racing through the screen door. He followed on her heels, only to be stopped by Hank's solemn look as he sat in the corner of the living room. Instead of chasing after Mandy up the stairs, he treaded lightly into the living room and dropped down into the chair opposite Hank.

"You're looking a whole lot better than I've seen you of late."

"Feel a lot better, too. In some ways anyway."

Hank's gaze was steady on Beau. What he saw was regret. That was something he didn't see often in a man like Hank.

"I'm sorry," Hank said quietly.

"What for?"

"I should have never come between you the first time."

"It wouldn't have made a difference and you know it. She would have ended up hating both of us for not stopping her. She's happier this way."

"Do you believe that?"

Beau's sigh was heavy. He wanted to believe Mandy was happy. She'd said she was happy here with him. But she was still leaving.

"Is that why you asked me to come back?"

Hank shrugged. "Partly. There were a lot of things that needed to be said. A big part of me wanted her to know before I died that I was her father. 'Cept I couldn't bring myself to tell her. I guess I was hoping you'd—"

"I didn't tell her, Hank. I promised you eight years ago she'd never learn the truth from me or my father."

Hank shook his head. "I can't figure it out then."

"She's a smart woman."

"That she is. You going to let her get on that plane tomorrow?"

Beau tossed his straw hat to the end table. "I can't stop her from doing what she wants to do."

"What about you? They're saying I'm gonna heal up pretty good. Are you ready to hit the road again?"

"I guess now is as good a time as any for us to talk about that."

Mandy woke to the smell of bacon and the sounds of hands already hard at work out in the barnyard. Lifting her head off the pillow, she realized she'd have to hustle to make it to the airport on time.

She had gone through the motions of packing her clothes and the makeup she hadn't worn at all since she'd arrived at the ranch, the night before after she'd left Beau on the porch. She didn't want him to see the tears that were pushing their way out. She'd let her heartache out alone in her room and cried her tears into the pillow. She was going to miss him.

She'd known leaving Texas was going to be hard. She'd worry about Hank and Corrine. And her heart would ache for Beau Gentry yet again. Only this time it would be worse because she didn't love him with the innocence of a young schoolgirl anymore. Now she loved him with the heart of a woman who knew what love was all about and how it could fill your soul more than any career. Now she knew that deep love could give her riches like nothing else. Except, she'd have to live her life never sharing that love with Beau.

She dragged herself from underneath the sheets and quickly showered and dressed in a pair of jeans and a light cotton shirt. When she got home, the new clothes would get tucked away in a drawer, the boots would be buried in the back of her closet along with her cowboy hat. She wasn't a rodeo man's woman. She never had been. She'd have to tell herself that many times to get through the days to come.

And she'd have to remind herself that she'd learned to live without Beau Gentry's love once before. She could do it again. She only hoped that this time she'd listen.

Breakfast was on the table and hands were barreling through the kitchen door when Mandy climbed down the stairs with her suitcase.

"Ya'll ready to go?" Hank asked.

She bent down and kissed his cheek. "In a few. I just need to give you and Aunt Corrine a couple more hugs and kisses to last me until I see you next."

"Ah, doll, make it soon," Corrine said, giving her a quick hug. "Now you sit down and eat some breakfast before you run off."

"The flight serves a meal."

"Ugh," Hank said. "You passing up Corrine's hotcakes for some airplane slop?"

"If I eat much more of Aunt Corrine's food I won't be able to fit into my jeans," she said, trying to sound lighthearted when she felt anything but. All the while she checked the doors for signs of Beau. The other hands were already hard at work on their breakfast. There was no sign of Beau.

She listened to the sounds filtering in from the window from the yard. No whistling. No boots clopping against the hard earth.

Hank took her by the hand. "There's time, darlin'. Sit and have some coffee at least."

She did as she was told. She talked about old times and days to come. She promised that she'd be coming back to the ranch again in a few months to go riding with Hank on the cattle drive. Her first. And as she said good-bye and the other hands ran out the door, her heart felt a heaviness and a renewed sense of hope all at the same time. There were tears and a lot of laughter when Beau finally appeared in the doorway.

"If we're going to make the flight, we should be going." His voice was deep with the same heaviness she felt inside. Without looking at her, he reached down for her bags and spun out the door.

"You call me as soon as you get home, you hear?" Corrine said, kissing her one last time on the cheek.

"I will." She gave a few extra seconds to Hank's hug, then said good-bye to both of them.

She was relieved when she walked out onto the porch that the other hands had made themselves scarce. Beau was standing beside his truck, the passenger door already open.

Taking a long look around the ranch and the hills beyond the pasture, she realized she was going to miss the Double T. Beau had asked her endlessly if she was happy in Philadelphia. She had to wonder how she could have thought she was ever happy there when being here with Beau gave her the greatest joy she could ever imagine. She had to wonder, too, if she'd feel that same happiness if she were here without him.

No, she told herself. She wouldn't think of what-if's or could-be's now. She was going home. Where she belonged. And Beau was going to ride out of Texas on another sunset without her. This time, she wouldn't watch him go. That much she was sure of.

"You ready?" Beau asked.

"I'm ready."

She climbed into the cab of the truck and secured her seat belt. A stab of pain pierced her heart and made her eyes swell with tears. Hank and Corrine would be standing together in the doorway of the porch. Mandy didn't have to turn around to know they were there. She felt it.

Fixing her sight on the driveway ahead, she braced herself for what was sure to be a long and painful ride. She immediately regretted agreeing to let Beau drive her all the way to the airport. She should have told him to drop her off at the bus station and suddenly wondered if she'd make her flight if he did that now.

She was mulling over the best way to tell him just that when the truck suddenly rolled to a stop at the front gate of the Double T.

She snapped her gaze to Beau as he jammed the truck into park.

"What's going on? Why are we stopping?"

Beau didn't say a word. Instead, he flung the driver's side door open and strode around the front of the truck to her side, opening the door.

"Come on," he finally said, taking her hand.

Undoing her seatbelt, she slid out of the cab without a word. Holding his hand, she followed him up a small incline that gave a picture-perfect view of the ranch and the hills beyond.

Silently, he turned her around so her back was snug against his chest, and he wrapped his arms around her, resting his chin on her shoulder.

"It's beautiful, isn't it?"

"Yes," she answered, swallowing the hard lump in her throat.

"You built a life without me back in Philadelphia," he whispered. "I can understand that. But I want you to know that when I'm holding you like this, or even looking at you from across the yard, I'm the happiest I think I've ever been in my life. What I feel for you is like nothing I've ever felt before. Nothing I've ever known in my life."

Her bottom lip trembled, and she didn't trust herself to speak.

"Spending these last few weeks here at the Double T has brought me face to face with a lot more than you, Mandy Morgan," Beau said.

"What are you talking about?"

"About us, about life. I never understood what Hank meant about roaming and coming home until now."

"Beau—"

"No, Mandy, listen to me. I've been thinking about what you said about my father. I don't think it will do a bit of good but I'm at least going to give it a try and that's a start."

"I'm glad," she said, tears stinging her eyes.

"There's more and you have to hear it before you go."

She craned her neck to look up at him and he kissed her forehead. She turned back to the horizon, to the ranch and all it had given her.

He was silent for what seemed like an eternity. She could feel his heart pounding against her back.

"You still steal my breath away. I can't let go of you," he whispered, his voice thick with emotion.

*Then don't let me go, Beau.* She wanted to say the words, wanted to tell him they'd find a way to work it out so they could be together. If only. . . .

"I have a plane to catch," she said, trying to pull free from his arms.

But Beau held onto her tighter. "There are other planes."

"Not today."

"Then tomorrow. Stay with me today. There'll be another one tomorrow."

"And rodeos?"

He shook his head. "No, no more rodeos."

"Of course there will be."

"It's time for me to stop and settle in some-where. I know I could just as easily go back to working the ranch with my father, but in the end nothing will change. He'll still hate not owning the Double T . . . and he'll hate that I'm desperately in love with the enemy's daughter."

"What did you say?"

He turned to her, framing her face with his hands. "I love you, Mandy. More than anything. I'm not letting you leave here without you being absolutely sure of that fact. I love you."

More than rodeo and the World Champion-ship? she wondered. He hadn't said it, but she saw the answers to all her unspoken question shining in the depths of his eyes. He did love her more than all the rest. This time she was sure of it.

"I'm done roaming. I've found the thing that is more important to me than rodeo. You. And this is where I want to be, right here with my arms around you."

He reached out and grazed her cheek with his fingers, sending shooting sparks flying in every direction.

"And I'm hoping one day this is where you'll want to be too."

"Oh, Beau," she whispered. "Why now?"

"Why not now when it matters most. When there's nothing holding us back. You said yourself people don't say what's truly in their hearts until it's too late. I don't know how to tell you what I'm feeling. I only know I don't want it to be too late."

"It's already too late. It won't change anything. You say you're done roaming. But pretty soon, you'll be itching to rodeo again. And what about me? I have friends, and a great job and . . . and . . . a life somewhere else. In Philadelphia. None of that fits in with rodeoing."

"I hear you. And I heard everything you said last night, too. You've built a life without me. But you could have a life here, too, and a man who loves you more than life itself.

"I'm just asking you to think about it. That's all. Go back to Philadelphia and live your life and if you're happy there, then fine. I'll have to accept it. But if you're not, then know I'm going to be right here waiting for you."

"You're really going to throw away the World Championship? You're not leaving?"

He shook his head. "It doesn't mean a whole lot without you."

"You're staying at the ranch?"

"I worked it out with Hank last night. We're going to start a rodeo school. I'll get to do what I love and be home every single night to share with you, if that's what you want. I'll wait as long as I have to to win your heart back again, Mandy. And when I do, I'm going to ask you to be my wife."

Her lips trembled. He loved her. Beau really and truly loved her and he wanted to marry her. Oh, God, what was she going to do?

She pulled out of his arms and walked a few steps away from him. She needed the distance to give her some clarity, to make her head stop spinning and keep her mind thinking straight. But all she wanted to do was turn around and launch herself into Beau's arms and never leave.

*He loved her.* After all the pain of thinking it was over, could she trust his love enough to open her heart again?

"Why aren't you asking me now?"

"You said you wanted to go back. I want you to be happy more than anything and you said—"

"I know what I said. I've been saying a lot these past few days. Now I want to hear it from you. Again."

A slow smile tipped the corner of his lips. Lord, how she loved that smile.

"I love you, Mandy. More than anything. I'm asking you to give me your heart, stay here with me, and be my wife."

"No more leaving?"

He opened his arms wide. "No more leaving."

She was in his arms before she could even think about anything else. And she knew without a doubt she could spend all her days happy and content right there as long as she had Beau to love. As long as she was in his heart and in his arms. They'd make it work.

She kissed him on the lips and gazed up at him with renewed hope and deep love. "Beau, there has never been anyone else but you. You've always had my heart. All you had to do was ask."

## LAKE COUNTY PUBLIC LIBRARY
## INDIANA

Some materials may be renewable by phone or in person if there are
no reserves or fines due.  www.lakeco.lib.in.us     LCP#0390